# THE RELUCTANT RUNAWAY

# THE RELUCTANT RUNAWAY

**JEFFREY
ARCHER
NESBIT**

## VICTOR BOOKS

A DIVISION OF SCRIPTURE PRESS PUBLICATIONS INC.
USA CANADA ENGLAND

THE CAPITAL CREW SERIES
*Crosscourt Winner*
*The Lost Canoe*
*The Reluctant Runaway*
*Struggle with Silence*

Cover illustration by Kathy Kulin-Sandel

**Library of Congress Cataloging-in-Publication Data**
Nesbit, Jeffrey Asher.
    The reluctant runaway / Jeffrey Asher Nesbit.
        p.    cm. — (The Capital crew series)
    Summary: In further adventures of the James family, Karen decides to run away to stay with her derelict alcoholic father, who has left the family.
    ISBN 0-89693-131-5
    [1. Family life—Fiction. 2. Christian life—Fiction.]
I. Title.    II. Series.
PZ7.N4378Re   1991
[Fic]—dc20                                                            91-9624
                                                                         CIP
                                                                         AC

1  2  3  4  5  6  7  8  9  10  Printing/Year  95  94  93  92  91

VICTOR BOOKS
A division of SP Publications, Inc.
Wheaton, Illinois 60187

To Elizabeth, who already seems to believe that everything is possible.

"For with God, nothing will be impossible" (Luke 1:37).

Thank you for your bright eyes and courage.

**I didn't really notice the first time** Karen was late for dinner. I'm almost always late for dinner. So's Chris. Usually we're late together, which makes it easier to face Mom.

Chris and I have it down pat. We'll notice that we're late, again, and we'll start tearing for the house. We both rip through the front door at the same time, skid into the turn at the kitchen, and take our seats at the same time.

Usually, Mom just glares at us. Then she shakes her head slowly. Then she cocks her head towards the oven. "It's on," she'll say. "Why don't you two warm up your plates?"

But not that night. Mom wasn't paying us the slightest bit of attention when we came hauling through the door, fifteen minutes late as usual. She was staring at Karen's empty seat, a slightly concerned frown creasing her face.

"Have either of you seen Karen?" she asked us both after a little while.

Chris shook his head. "Nope," I answered. Chris and I had been playing "murder" basketball and we hadn't really been paying much attention to anything other than our own well being.

You see, "murder" basketball isn't the kind of sport that lets you keep track of your sister while you're playing. It takes everything you have just to stay in the game.

I don't know who really started the game in our neighborhood. I think somebody saw it on cable or something. The idea is simple—you play basketball without any rules. The object is to score, if you can make it through the gang tackles, trips, and head-knocking forearms.

"You're sure?" Mom asked.

"Mom, we haven't seen her all day," Chris said.

"Yeah, she left this morning," I said. "She didn't say where she was going." I glanced over at Jana, expectantly.

"She didn't tell me, either," Jana said. "She just left."

"That's strange," Mom murmured, more to herself than to us. "Not a word. And late for dinner."

"So what?" Susan said, making a face at me. "Cally's late all the time. His dinner's always cold."

"Who asked you?" I said, making a face back at her. She stuck her tongue out at me. I reached across the table and grabbed for it. She jerked back, giggling, and almost fell out of her chair.

"Not even close," she said to me.

"Next time," I vowed.

"You're too slow," she teased.

"You'll see," I said ominously.

Susan refused to yield. "You're still always late. You're never home in time for dinner."

"That's not true," I protested. "I make it most of the time."

"No way," Susan said, crinkling her nose at me. "I'll bet you're late most of the time."

"What's the bet?" I asked, my heart sinking slightly. I hoped she didn't take me up.

"Clean my room for a week?" she offered.

I thought about it for a second. Susan always kept her room spotless, so hers would be a breeze to keep clean. Mine, on the other hand, wasn't suitable for a pigsty. It was an easy bet.

"You're on," I said.

Instinctively, Susan and I both glanced at John, who could settle most disputes, if you asked him about it the right way. He couldn't really remember concepts forever. But this was right up his alley.

John, in his own abstract way, had been following the argument. He almost knew my question before I asked it. He's like that. He anticipates me. I'm always challenging him with something, and he lies in wait for the questions.

"Just weekdays, or the whole week?" John asked me.

"Weekdays," I said, hoping Susan didn't protest. I was more apt to be punctual during the week, because I wanted to see Mom when she got off work.

"Uh-uh," Susan said. "The whole week."

John nodded, and filed the information into his computer brain. "For the past month, or for the whole year?"

I thought about it for a second. It had been about a month since Chris and I had come home from summer camp and our three-day "adventure" in the woods. I'd been pretty slack about getting home on time since then.

"Better make it since January," I said.

"You were late for dinner 127 times," John said an instant later.

I couldn't add so fast, but I knew I was in trouble. "And I was on time . . . ?"

"Just sixty-four times," John said, the barest trace of a smile on his face. He loved watching me go down in defeat.

I groaned. Susan was beaming from ear to ear. You can't argue with John. He's never wrong, not about statistics. I don't know how he does it, but he remembers things like this. I'd just have to accept my fate.

"You don't really have to clean my room, Cally," offered Susan.

"I'll clean your dumb room," I growled. "Just don't go out of your way to make any big messes."

"Oh, I won't," Susan said brightly. I knew she didn't care whether I actually cleaned her room. She was just happy she'd beaten me.

I glanced over at Mom. She hadn't really been paying a whole lot of attention to any of us. She had one eye on the telephone and the other on the front door, which she could just barely see from the kitchen.

"Hey, Jana, you're *sure* you don't know where Karen might be?" I asked.

Jana shook her head. "I asked her if she wanted to go to the pool with me, but she said she had some stuff to do."

"What kind of stuff?" I asked.

"Just stuff. She didn't say."

I wondered for a second if maybe Jana wasn't holding back, protecting her twin sister. They were like that. They protected each other. It was the only time

Jana ever really kept secrets.

But Jana seemed genuinely baffled, so I didn't press her. She'd just get mad, and that wouldn't do anyone a bit of good.

I heard the car door slam almost at the same time Mom did. But she was out of her seat a split second before I'd shoved mine back from the table. Mom could move pretty fast when she wanted to.

She was staring out the window right next to the front door when I arrived. I stepped beside her and looked out as well, just in time to see a big, ugly, rusted-out Buick of some sort roar away down the street. It needed a new muffler, or at least a muffler of some sort.

"She got out of the car?" I asked. Mom just nodded. "Who do you think it was? A boyfriend?"

We both watched Karen walk up the walkway slowly. She was obviously lost in thought. As she got closer, I could see that she'd been crying. There were tear streaks down both sides of her face.

"No, I don't think it was a boyfriend," Mom said.

"Then who was it?" I asked.

Mom didn't answer, and Karen came through the door an instant later. She glanced at the two of us, almost burst out crying again, and then bolted up the stairs to her bedroom.

I started to follow Mom up the stairs to Karen's bedroom, but she put a hand on my shoulder gently. "Why don't you go back to the dinner table with the rest of the kids?" she suggested.

"But I . . . "

"Please, Cally," she insisted. "I'd like to talk to Karen."

I looked at Mom for a moment or two before it finally dawned on me who'd been in that crummy car. I should have known right away. It was my crummy father. That's why Karen was crying. I was sure of it.

"Okay," I sighed, wishing for the zillionth time that I had a different dad, and knowing that I was sort of stuck with the one I had.

I watched Mom troop slowly up the stairs to talk to her daughter, and then turned toward the kitchen. I arrived not a moment too soon. Timmy had just nailed Susan with one of his peas, and my youngest sister was about to retaliate with a Ritz cracker.

**Mom wouldn't talk after she came downstairs.**
She just shook her head when I asked her silently,
with raised eyebrows, for an explanation. I shrugged,
and went back to refereeing.

If they had a game show called "Family Squabble,"
where the object was to do crummy things to members of your own family, we'd be the world champi-
ons. No question about it.

Inspired by Timmy, Chris had managed to avoid eating his own peas by dumping half of them down Susan's back before I could intervene. The other half
were now either smushed on the floor or rolling
around under someone's chair.

Susan continued the game, of course, by applying
some of her mashed potatoes to John's hair. Poor John
never even knew what hit him. To his credit, though,
he built a miniature launching pad with his knife,
plate, and spoon and lobbed a dozen peas back at
Susan.

Even Jana, who usually stays out of everything, got
in the middle of this one. Timmy thought it was really
quite funny when Susan tossed a pea at Jana; he
promptly tipped his plate over into Jana's lap.

I tried to stop all of this, I really did. But no one

actually listens to me. I'm not their dad, after all. I'm just their dumb, older brother who makes as many mistakes as they do.

It stopped all right when Mom came back, but the damage had been done. Dinner was a disaster, and I seriously doubt whether a great deal of it was eaten.

Jana slipped away quietly somewhere in the middle. There one minute, gone the next. Jana was like that. When she wanted to, she could just go about her business.

I knew where she'd gone. Up to see Karen. They'd talk about it, because they didn't have any secrets between them, and then somehow I'd have to pry it out of Jana. It wouldn't be easy.

The two of them were huddled together in their room for an awfully long time, though, so I finally gave up waiting for Jana and headed outside with Chris.

Chris and I were continuing our marathon whiffle ball game. I was up 276 to 189, but Chris was surging. He'd scored 34 runs in the last two days to my lousy 11. I'd been coasting. Now, I had to start getting serious again if I wanted to hold Chris off.

We had a pretty nice setup in the backyard. The batter stood with his back to the house, which didn't sound so great *inside* the house when the ball smacked up against it, but sure did keep the ball from skidding away from us all the time.

And we had a neighbor family's fence as the home run boundary, which was great except when their golden retriever stole the ball and we had to chase him around forever to get the ball back, and then clean all the drool off of it.

Chris had really been crunching my fastball lately,

so I was throwing all sorts of junk at him—knuckle-balls that dropped into the ground, curves that broke about three feet, and risers that sometimes took off and headed for his ear. Chris hated my junk.

"You're a big sissy throwing that stuff!" he hissed at me after one especially wicked curve forced him out of the batter's box and then broke cleanly over the plate and smacked up against the "strike" zone I'd etched onto the house with some white chalk.

Mom, by the way, was not real thrilled with that move. The chalk, I mean. I told her not to worry, that the chalk was on the back side of the house, where no one could see it, and that I could always wash it off if I had to. She didn't buy it, not for a second.

"No guts," I crowed, reveling in the fact that Chris wouldn't stay in the box against my curve.

"Oh, give me a break," Chris glowered. "You're the one who's chicken. You won't throw me a fastball."

"I'm not chicken," I countered. "I just mix my pitches up, that's all. And you can't hit 'em."

"Oh, yeah? Well, why don't you try a fastball every now and then, see what I do with that?" Chris taunted.

"You wouldn't touch it."

"Try me."

"Maybe I will."

"No, you won't. You're a chicken. *And* a sissy."

I knew Chris was just baiting me, hoping I'd throw him a fastball. Well, maybe I would, just to prove to him that I wasn't a sissy, or a chicken. I'd just blow one right by him and that would settle it.

I went into my windup. Chris got set in the box. I unloaded. The ball was smoking as it screamed towards the plate. Chris started his swing almost at the same time the ball left my hand.

And then he crushed it. The ball sailed, sailed, sailed and disappeared deep into the neighbors' yard. It was, by far, the longest home run he'd ever hit off of me. No doubt about it.

"Yes!" he said, one fist raised high in glory. "Yes! A *monster* home run! A Guinness Book shot!"

I glared at him. I was trying to think of some wonderful, cutting response. None immediately sprang to mind. He'd murdered my fastball, pure and simple.

"Lucky," I finally managed to murmur.

"Lucky?" he snorted. "You kiddin'? I *killed* that ball. You may never find it. And if you do, it probably has a big dent in it."

"You're still down by 86 runs," I said lamely.

"Yeah, and so what? Keep throwing me fastballs and I'll catch up in a hurry," he boasted.

I turned and headed towards the neighbors' yard. Chris was almost right. It took me a few minutes to find the ball. It had rolled all the way up to their house and under the bushes. I didn't tell that to Chris, of course. No way. He'd gloat about it for days if I told him.

Instead, I came back and threw him a knuckleball, a curve, and a change-up, in that order. He struck out, badly, on the change-up.

But Chris didn't even seem to mind. He was still savoring the Herculean home run he'd clobbered off me. I'd probably still be hearing about it a week from now.

**I finally cornered Jana in the kitchen,** after Timmy, Susan, and John had gone to bed. She looked tired and drained. Karen must really have been upset.

"So what's the deal?" I asked Jana, deciding the direct approach might work best.

"So nothin'," she answered, not even glancing at me. She opened the refrigerator door and started to scrounge around for something to eat. Fat chance of that. Chris had cleaned out all the good stuff.

"So are you gonna tell me what's goin' on or not?" I asked, knowing for certain now that this really would not be easy.

" 'Bout what?" Jana asked, her head deep in the refrigerator. She was poking around in the back, behind the mayonnaise, pickle relish, and leftover tomato sauce.

Boy, was that a waste of time. I'd been back in that part of the refrigerator at least three times. The only thing left back there was a half-eaten dill pickle, a couple of really soggy peach slices, and a banana that was undoubtedly pitch-black by now.

"Come on! You know," I said, a little exasperated. She was making this more difficult than she had to.

Jana emerged from the refrigerator with a scowl.

"Isn't there anything to eat around this place?"

"Nope," I said, chuckling. "Chris and John wiped it out two days ago, and Mom hasn't gone to the store yet."

"There has to be something," Jana said, attacking the produce drawers now with a vengeance. I already knew what she'd find there as well—a dried-up apple, a bunch of wilted lettuce, some bean sprouts that would *never* get eaten, and a stalk of celery that had been there for a century at least.

"You're not going to tell me, are you? You've signed some blood pact with Karen, haven't you?"

I heard a little giggle from somewhere deep within the refrigerator. "A blood pact?"

"Yeah, you probably took a really sharp knife, cut your little toe with it, and then pledged not to tell a soul about your secret."

"That sounds like somethin' you'd do with your dopey friends," Jana said. She'd given up on the fridge. Now she was combing through the freezer. That was an equally barren wasteland as well.

Jana was really being evasive. And it wasn't just because she was looking for something to eat. She really must have told her twin that she wouldn't tell what was going on. I'd have to try another tactic.

"Okay, I give up," I sighed. "But can you at least tell me this? Is Dad in town for good, or did he just come up to visit?"

"How do you know Dad's here?" she asked sharply, pausing in her futile search for nourishment.

"Because I *saw* him, for cryin' out loud," I scowled. "I saw Karen leaving that ratty old Buick he has now."

"You don't know that was him," Jana said.

" 'Course I do," I said boldly. "Now, would you just tell me already? Is he in town for good?"

Jana glared at me for a couple of seconds, then she shook her head. *Good,* I thought. *I at least got that out of her.* Jana went back to the freezer. I thought about my next question.

"But he came up to see Karen, is that it? He figured she was such a soft touch, he'd just worm his way back into the family through her?"

Jana jerked her head out of the freezer and whirled on me. I knew that would get her. She'd defend her sister to the death, and I had just tossed something in her path that she couldn't sidestep.

"She's not like that and you know it, Cally!" Jana said angrily. "I mean, what's she supposed to do? Just ignore Dad the way you always do?"

"I don't ignore him," I answered. "I just don't want him around. He hurt Mom, and I don't think he's sorry about it."

"He is too sorry!" Jana blurted out.

I had her now. "Oh, you gotta be kiddin' me," I said. "No way is he sorry. I can tell. He just wants back in the family because he messed up and now he doesn't know what to do—"

"He *is* sorry about it, Cally," Jana said again. "He really is. Dad knows that he really did something rotten. He just wants to say he's sorry. And Mom won't even listen to him."

Now I was starting to get angry. "Mom won't listen to him?" I asked, my voice rising in pitch. "Are you crazy, Jana? That's all Mom did her whole life. She listened to every crummy, rotten thing Dad said. Mom's the world champion listener."

"Not right now, she isn't," Jana persisted. I don't think she really believed what she was saying. I could almost hear Karen's voice as Jana spoke. It was Karen who believed this about our lousy father, not Jana.

"Can you blame her?" I asked. "After what he did—leaving the family and running away with a girl half his age?"

"It was a mistake. He knows that now," Jana insisted. "He was just goin' through a really bad time, losin' his job and all."

"I'll tell you what the mistake was," I said viciously, moving a little closer to Jana. "It was a mistake comin' back here. He should never have done that— not to see Karen, or me or Mom or anyone. *That* was the mistake."

"Karen doesn't think so," Jana said softly, clutching the refrigerator door for all it was worth. "She loves Dad. We all do. Even you, Cally."

I felt like beating my fist against the wall. I wanted to just pound something, anything. I didn't know what I thought. It wasn't that I hated Dad. It was just that I loved Mom so much, and he had really hurt her so deeply. I didn't think I could ever forget that. Not ever.

"Dad should just stay away," I said through clenched teeth. "He shouldn't come back. I don't *care* what Karen says. He had his chance, and he blew it."

"But he's back, Cally, and there's nothin' you can do about it," Jana said, her eyes brimming red.

"There is too something I can do about it," I said defiantly.

"No, there isn't, and you know it," she said. "Karen says Dad just wants to talk to Mom, that's all. He just wants to say he's sorry and ask her to forgive him."

"Yeah, and Mom would probably forgive him," I said bitterly.

"So what's wrong with that?" Jana asked, genuinely perplexed at my raw anger towards Dad. It must have seemed like an open wound to her.

"Because he hasn't really changed, that's why," I said. "He'll just ask Mom to forgive him, then he'll just do it all over again. All that yellin' and cussin' and stuff. He hasn't changed."

"Maybe he has," Jana said. "Karen says he has, that he's a *lot* different than he was before."

"Yeah, well, I think Karen's wrong. She's just dead wrong. Dad hasn't changed. I just know it."

Jana finally found something, deep, deep within the freezer, half-stuck beneath some very frozen hamburger patties at the bottom of the last freezer bin. She held up the frozen yogurt stick proudly, peeled off the wrapper, and jammed it in her mouth.

"You always think you're so smart, Cally," Jana said as she cracked off a bite. "But you don't know everything. You just don't."

Maybe. I guess it was possible that even Dad could change. But I really doubted it. *There are people you just gotta watch out for in life. You just have to keep your eye on them all the time, to make sure you always know what they're up to. And my father is one of them.*

"I just hope Karen doesn't get hurt," I said finally, staring glumly at the yogurt stick Jana had found, wondering how I'd overlooked such a treasure in my own searches.

"Karen knows what she's doin'," Jana said confidently. "She really does."

"I hope so," I said over my shoulder as I started to rummage through the freezer myself, wondering what other morsels might be buried in there. "I really do."

**4**

**It was dangerous at the net** with the six-year-olds. Not life threatening or anything like that, but a little scary sometimes.

The six-year-olds had just enough "oomph" on the ball to zip it across the net, but they never knew where the ball was going. Or, at least, *I* didn't know where it was going.

So I'd stand up there at the net and lob balls at them, and they'd fire it right back—sometimes into the net, sometimes off the ceiling, and sometimes off the water cooler.

What's worse, they liked to help me gather up the balls when they were scattered all over the place. "Here, Mr. James," one of them would call and fire it right at my head. I'd duck, of course, and the ball would roll three courts down at the club.

And I thought teaching kids how to play tennis would be fun.

Well, actually, in a way, it's not so bad. I don't mind getting a tennis ball in the ear every so often. Really, I don't. The kids I was teaching that summer at the indoor tennis club where I worked part-time were fun to watch.

Most of them learned so quickly. They'd pick stuff

up right away. It didn't take much to teach them. They just soaked everything up the way a towel picks water up off the floor.

I really got a kick out of watching a kid who could barely hold the racket at first "suddenly" begin to fire backhands across the net. It didn't take much. Just a little self-confidence, a little inspiration, and the right grip on the racket.

I guess I didn't really think of myself as a teacher. I wasn't teaching these kids anything. I was just showing them what I'd learned, most of it through my own trial and error. They were getting the benefit of learning from my mistakes.

Which is the way it should be, I guess. There's no law I know of that says we have to learn everything the hard way, that we can't let people who've already made those mistakes guide us past the jagged rocks that always threaten to wreck us.

"Cally, my old pal, wanna hit some?"

I didn't even have to turn around. I almost instantly recognized the whining, slightly nasal, and always sarcastic voice. There was no other like it in the world. "Sure," I said, turning to face my old archenemy, Evan Grant, who was leaning casually against the plate-glass window that looked out over the six courts at the indoor tennis club.

Evan gave me one of his smart aleck grins. "You know you don't stand a chance against me at the indoor nationals this winter?"

I laughed. Evan never let up. He'd also never forget that I'd beaten him this past winter to win the national indoor tennis championships in the 12-and-under age-group.

"I don't think I'm your problem this year, Evan," I said. "We gotta go up against the 14-year-olds, and I hear there are a whole bunch of 'em who are terrific."

"Ah, we can handle *them*," he sneered. "No problem."

"I dunno," I said, shaking my head. *"Tennis* magazine says that a few of them are showing signs of heading straight into the pro ranks . . ."

"What do they know?" Evan said. "Just a bunch of writers sitting around on their duffs who've probably never played anybody half as good as you or me."

"Maybe you're right."

"I *know* I am."

It was funny, but I couldn't help myself. I was starting to like Evan Grant. I was almost beginning to like his complete arrogance, his almost incessant cockiness, his disdain for the common things of life. It was refreshing. It energized me. It also infuriated me.

Evan's family had more money than I could even imagine. He was a direct descendant of President Grant, the Civil War hero. Me, I'm a direct descendant of Jesse James, the crummy outlaw.

He had six tennis rackets to my one. He had tailored tennis clothes. Mine came from a discount department store. He rode to the tennis club in expensive cars. I rode to it on my bike.

Yet we had the same drive, the same ambition to be the best tennis players in the world. Or, at least, the best tennis players in whatever arena we happened to be in. That was what locked us in mortal combat, despite our vast differences.

"So are you gonna hit, or what?" he asked, tossing a tennis ball at my head.

I caught it six inches from me and fired it right back. Evan caught the return without flinching. "Let's go," I said, and grabbed my racket.

As we walked down to the courts, I suddenly decided to let Evan in on what had been nagging at me for a day now, ever since I'd talked to Jana. I couldn't believe I was actually telling Evan Grant anything. Only two months ago, we couldn't say a civil word.

"My dad's back in town," I said quietly as we walked down the steps.

Evan glanced at me sharply, instantly reading the pain on my face. "Too bad," he said. "From what you've told me, he sounds like a real loser. You're better off without him."

I winced. But Evan was cutting right to the bone, just as he always does. He never fools around. He always gets right to it, even though it hurts sometimes. Maybe that's what I really like about him.

"I just can't think that way," I said. "He's my dad."

"I guess. But you guys—your family, I mean—are doing all right up here in D.C. Why doesn't he just leave you alone?"

"Beats me," I said, half-wishing that I could turn Evan loose on my father. That would be interesting to watch.

"You oughta just tell him to get out of town," Evan said firmly. "Really. Just tell the creep to take a hike. He can't just walk back into your life and wreck everything again."

"I don't *know* that he'd wreck everything."

"Oh, give me a break, would ya? He'd leech and mooch off you big-time, and then he'd run at the first chance he got."

"Maybe not," I protested halfheartedly.

"You're dreamin', Cally," Evan said. "Which isn't like you."

It was almost the first nice thing Evan had ever said about me. "But he's my *dad,* Evan," I answered. "I can't just walk away."

"Sure you can. Who's gonna stop you? Just tell him you don't want him around anymore. You're better off when he's just a memory."

We tossed our warm-ups off to the side. Evan cracked a new can of balls. That meant we were in for a whale of a match. New balls jumped. I'd have to stay on my toes.

"I can't do that," I said finally, realizing for perhaps the first time that I really didn't want my father back. Even though Evan's words hurt, he was right. Our family was probably better off without him. He wouldn't change. At least I didn't think he would.

"You can, if you want," Evan said.

"No, I can't," I said firmly. "He's my father, and the Bible says you have to honor your parents. I have to do that. I don't have a choice."

Evan stared at me. He hated it when I talked about the Bible. He listened, but it sort of drove him crazy. "I know you believe in all that stuff, Cally. But there's gotta be something in the Bible that says you can tell rotten, crummy skunks like your father to take a hike."

"Maybe," I said, smiling for the first time since I'd learned my father was back in town. "But honoring your parents is one of the Ten Commandments. You know, the tablets Moses brought down from the mountain—"

"I know what the Ten Commandments are!" Evan

snapped. "But there has to be something in there about lousy fathers who abandon their families—"

"I don't think so," I laughed. "But I'll look." I grabbed the yellow ball as Evan bounced it my direction. It was still crisp and new and fresh, not all fuzzed-up from getting whacked around.

Sort of like my father when he was young, before he'd had seven kids and been laid off from his job at the steel mill. *Surely,* I thought, *my father was a great guy once. . . . He was, wasn't he? A neat guy, somebody Mom could fall in love with?*

I took the first ball Evan lobbed in my direction and crunched it viciously, hoping against reason perhaps that my real father would come back, the one Mom had gotten married to once upon a time. I didn't think it would happen.

*God, I need help with this one,* I prayed. *I don't understand how I can live up to Your commandment, and still think the way I do about my father. The two don't go together. And I don't know how to make them fit.*

Evan blistered one down the line. Even though it was only practice, I was still embarrassed that I was way out of position. *Time to get back to work,* I thought. *Time to get back to the task at hand.* I took the next ball and drilled it crosscourt. Evan barely got his racket on it.

My father would just have to wait. I had a job to do right now. I'd think about him later.

**It must be murder on my mom.** As if seven kids weren't enough for anyone to handle, she'd decided soon after we'd moved to Washington, D.C. that she really wanted to pass the Foreign Service exam.

What made it so tough was that the only time she could ever study for it was at night, after the younger kids were sound asleep. And, of course, by then she was so dead tired she could barely keep her eyes open.

But Mom had a will of iron. She was determined to do this, even if it never led to anything like a neat, new job somewhere. It was a test she just felt like she absolutely had to pass.

I was almost afraid to ask her why she was so determined. She still needed to get her college diploma before passing the Foreign Service exam would really mean something. There were a lot of very tall hurdles still in her path.

But nothing ever seemed to rattle or shake my mom. Except my dad, when he was on a rampage. But he was gone, at least for the time being.

I saw Karen later that night, after my practice session with Evan Grant. Evan had beaten me in three sets, two to one. But it was okay. The third set had gone to a tiebreaker, and I'd played well. It was only practice, and we'd both gotten a lot out of it.

Karen was in the bathroom, throwing cold water on her face, when I saw her. Her face was all puffy. Her eyes were red. It was obvious, even to me, that she'd been crying. She'd probably been on the phone with Dad.

I must have stopped and stared. Suddenly, Karen looked up, and our eyes met. "What are you lookin' at?" she asked.

"Nothing," I mumbled, looking away.

"Better not be," she said.

"Hey, don't worry. It's your life."

"What's that supposed to mean?" Karen said, drying her face off with a towel. She emerged from the bathroom, clearly aching for a fight. I had half a mind to give her one.

"It doesn't mean anything. I don't care what you do."

Karen glared at me. She was clearly torn. Part of her wanted to just lay into me, as if I was to blame for the predicament she now found herself in. And part of her wanted to confide in me, as she'd done so many times in the past when she just wanted to talk.

The fighter won. "He's your dad too, you know," she said defiantly. "Or maybe you've forgotten already?"

"He doesn't act like one," I countered.

"Why don't you just give him a chance. Maybe he will."

I laughed. "Yeah, sure. He had his chance . . . "

"He wants another one. He's different, Cally, he really is. He's changed."

I started to walk away. I didn't want to hear this. I

knew Dad hadn't changed, not really. He was just scared now, and we were all he had left.

"If he's changed so much," I said, pausing, looking back over my shoulder at Karen, "how come he doesn't just come up to the door and show us all what a great guy he is?"

"Because *you* won't let him," Karen said. "And Mom won't."

"*I* won't let him? That's just crazy. I'm not standin' in his way."

"He says you are," Karen said. "He says you and Mom are just set against him, that you won't let him come back and show everybody that he's changed."

That floored me. "Karen, you know that isn't true," I said. "I couldn't keep Dad from coming back, even if I wanted to."

"Well, he says you're turnin' all the kids against him, that you and Mom are doing that."

I could see that Karen was actually beginning to believe this. And I didn't know what to do about it. "I'm not, and you know it," I said flatly, and walked away. I bolted down the stairs towards the kitchen. I could hear Karen following me down the stairs.

"Dad says he wants to talk to you," Karen called out after me.

"I don't want to talk to him," I answered.

Karen caught up with me in the hallway. "But why?" she asked, almost ready to burst into tears again. "He's your *dad.*"

"Is he? He walked away from us, or have you forgotten that already?" I kept walking, trying to get away from this argument. It was hopeless. I'd never be able to convince my sister.

I made it to the kitchen before Karen could say anything. She turned the corner, her mouth open like she was going to say something, and it was like she hit a brick wall.

Karen saw Mom, sitting at the kitchen table with her study books spread out in front of her, and she just stopped dead in her tracks. Her mouth snapped shut, her face a grim mask of unhappiness.

I knew Mom had heard us talking. But she wasn't letting on. Maybe that was just as well. If we got started now, we might end up fighting all night.

I sat down beside Mom and glanced over her shoulder. She was looking at something on the Middle East, something about the roots of the Palestinian problem. I waited to see if Karen would join us at the table.

She didn't. She just hovered at the edge of the kitchen, staring angrily in my direction. Boy, was she fuming. I could almost see the smoke coming out of her ears.

Finally, clearly in a huff, she whirled and stomped away. I could hear her heavy footsteps as they thudded up the stairs.

"You shouldn't do that, Cally," my mother said quietly. She didn't even look up from her books.

"Do what?"

"Bait your sister like that."

"But I wasn't doing anything," I protested.

"She's angry and she's hurt right now," Mom said. "You shouldn't argue with her just for the fun of it."

"But, Mom, she started it . . . "

She looked up then. "It's been awhile since I heard that excuse."

"What excuse?"

Mom screwed up her face, imitating one of us when we're complaining. "But she started it," she whined.

I grimaced. "Come on. I didn't sound like *that*."

"Almost," Mom smiled.

"All right, you don't need to rub it in," I sighed. "I'm trying not to fight with Karen."

"Good," Mom said, and turned back to her books.

"But it's not easy."

"Nothing in life ever is, Cally," Mom said. "But I think you already know that."

**I guess I always knew** I couldn't really avoid her. I'd managed to go the whole school year without getting together "just to talk," as she'd said. And then the summer had come, which meant another few months where I wouldn't see her.

But Elaine Cimons—with a "C"—was persistent. You had to give her that. She tracked me down, and finally called me.

"Are you ever *hard* to find in the phone book!" she said breathlessly over the phone.

"Why?" I said glumly, not sure what I felt at that moment.

"Why? Because there must be a million people in the world with the last name of James, and I think I've called half of them."

"Oh, I see," I said, sort of wishing I could just hang up right in the middle of the conversation. "I never thought about it."

"Come on! Whatcha mean you never thought about it? Doesn't anyone ever call you?"

"Sure, they call me."

"Well, anyway," Elaine said, "I've found you now."

I grimaced. It's a good thing you can't see that sort of thing over the telephone. I'd be in big trouble.

"Yeah, I guess you have," I mumbled.

"You know why I'm callin'?"

"Nope."

"I'm getting some people together, that's why!" she said brightly.

"Yeah?"

"I thought we could get together some over the summer and study one of the New Testament books, like maybe the Book of Acts, or maybe James."

"Hmmm."

"So are you gonna join us? We'll probably have the first meeting at my house, in a few days."

I closed my eyes, wishing I was somewhere else. Boy, was she persistent! Ever since I'd bumped into her in the hallway at school, knocking her books all over the place, I'd had this sinking feeling in my stomach.

I knew God put people in your path, to teach you things or to steer you toward things. Elaine Cimons seemed to be one of those people God was putting squarely in the middle of mine.

Elaine always wore a big, wooden cross in school. She carried these pamphlets around school and handed them out to kids. The pamphlets were actually pretty neat. They talked about why Jesus died on the cross for our sins, and stuff like that.

But she was so bubbly about it, so happy all the time. She seemed to smile almost nonstop. It made me feel like I wasn't doing something quite right, that my own Christian faith just wasn't quite up to what hers was.

I couldn't really blame Elaine for that. She'd tell me I was just being silly, that some people are just natur-

ally happy and others—like me—never seemed to
learn how to make their smiling muscles work.

That didn't mean I wasn't a good Christian. It just
meant I was terrible at smiling.

"Well?" she asked again.

"Well, what?"

"Are you gonna join us, be part of our group?"

"I, um, well . . ."

"It'll only be every couple of weeks," she said. "You
can make that, can't you?"

"I have tennis lessons and stuff," I offered.

"During the day, though, right?"

"Well, yeah."

"This would be at night, right after dinner."

"Oh."

"So I can count on you?"

"Well, I guess . . ."

"Great!" she said. "I just knew you'd join us."

"I'm pretty bad about reading stuff beforehand," I
said, still wondering how I'd gotten myself into this
mess.

"Oh, don't worry. You can always read the chapter
we'll be studying right before we start."

"I don't ever say much in groups."

"You won't have to. Quit worrying so much."

"And I'm pretty lousy at answering questions about
what I believe in or what I think about things . . ."

"Oh, Cally!" she bubbled. I could almost see that
buck-tooth grin of hers at the other end of the line.
"I've seen you play tennis. You're good at something,
when you want to be."

"Tennis is different. I don't have to say anything on
the court. I can just play."

"But that's a way of expressing yourself, you silly. It's just about the same thing as talking."

"Yeah, I guess I let my racket do the talking for me."

"There you go. See?"

Actually, no, I didn't. But I wasn't about to say anything now that might get me in deeper.

"So I guess you'll probably call me again, right? To let me know when you're gonna have this meeting?"

"I'll call you. Don't worry. It'll be fun."

Yeah, sure. About as much fun as studying for a math quiz, or maybe mowing the lawn.

 **7**

**The car was sitting deep in the shade,** well off the road. It was parked sort of cockeyed, with its back, right tire way off the gravel and part of the front bumper jutting out toward the road.

Normally, I wouldn't have noticed it. I usually don't see things until they're right in my face, and even then I'm likely to miss it.

But this car stuck out like a sore thumb, especially compared to the car I stepped from.

"See ya, Evan," I said, waving to my archenemy in the backseat of the huge, black Lincoln. "And thanks for the ride, Mr. Grant."

"My pleasure," Evan's dad said from the front seat. "And, Cally, don't protest so much the next time we offer you a ride home."

"But it's out of your way," I said, refusing to give up.

"No, it isn't, you moron," Evan said, shaking his head.

"He's right," his dad said. "We're just five minutes from here."

I stared at the two of them, wondering how I'd fallen into such company. Oh well. "Well, okay, thanks," I mumbled.

"Hey, Cally?" Evan said.

"Yeah?"

"You were lucky today. You know that, don't you?"

The grin about pushed my ears back. "No way. That wasn't luck. All skill."

Evan cocked one eye. "In your dreams, Cally. Next time, it'll be different."

"Yeah, next time you won't take a game off me in the last set."

Evan smiled, which isn't something he would even have been capable of a year ago. "I don't think so," he said quietly. "Your serve was on today. That's all. It might not be the next time."

Evan was right, actually. My serve *had* been on, and I'd been lucky. There was no way I'd ever beat Evan 6-1 in a set again. But I wasn't about to say so.

"We have to go," his dad interrupted. "Your mother's waiting."

"Okay," Evan said, and jabbed his left hand at the power window button. The window started to close in my face. "Next time," he vowed, right before it closed. I just shook my head at him as the car roared away, accelerating up the hill in front of our house.

That's when I spotted the old, rusted-out Buick parked deep in the shadows across the street, maybe three houses down. Spying on us, spying on me. My head spun, like it will when you've been out in the hot sun too long without something to eat or drink.

I turned to walk towards the house, my knees a little shaky. I'd taken a few steps when a cold, hard anger began to wrench at me. I wasn't letting him do this, not to me, not to my mom, not to Karen. At least not without a fight.

I turned on my heels and began the long, long walk down the road, to meet my father in his den.

As I approached the car, I was sure I saw him toss something in the backseat, over his shoulder.

The car really was ugly. I'm not sure a junk dealer would take it off my dad for a hundred bucks. The front bumper was slightly askew. There was a long crack in the front windshield. The paint was peeling everywhere. There was a big dent on the passenger side, and a long, nasty scrape mark where someone had sideswiped another car.

I could smell him from a good ten feet away. It wafted out the open windows of the car, even in the open air. But I was ready for it this time. I knew what to expect from him. I wasn't surprised, like I had been on the tennis court at the national indoor championships.

A quick glance in the backseat as I came up to the side of the car, on the passenger side, confirmed my guess. There had to be at least six empty beer cans in the backseat, not to mention a whole bunch of other junk like sandwich wrappers, half-eaten candy bars, and crumpled-up potato chip bags.

"Ridin' in style, I see," my father drawled, dragging out the vowels like he always does when he's drunk.

"Just a friend," I said, not batting an eye.

"Some friend. Oughta get cozy there," he growled.

I didn't say anything. That was the way my father thought: What can you get from somebody? What kind of life can you suck out of them?

"You make sure you get somethin' outta the deal, boy," my father continued.

"Yeah, like what?" I said, trying to lean casually on the door of the car. The window bit into my arm, but I just shifted position slowly, like I didn't have a care in the world.

"Just a little, ole piece o' the pie, that's all," he drawled. "That's all I ever want outta life. Just a piece o' the pie. I got it comin' to me. I'm *due.*"

I stared at my dad. He was pretty lousy drunk, even though it was only late afternoon. I guess he didn't have anything better to do. Some people watch soap operas to pass the time in the afternoon. My dad gets sploshed and spies on his own kids.

I closed my eyes for a brief moment and prayed for strength. I had none right now. This was much, much more than I'd bargained for.

"Whatcha doin', boy?" my dad barked. "Prayin'? That it?"

I opened my eyes slowly, glad I'd sent a silent prayer forward even if it brought down my dad's wrath. "Yes, I was," I said quietly.

"Just like your mom," he guffawed. "Thinkin' you're talkin' to God, when there ain't nobody there."

"God *is* there," I said. "All you have to do is ask Him. He'll answer."

"Yeah, sure," he snorted. "I asked Him 'bout a hundred times for things, and I ain't never seen a one of 'em show up on my doorstep. So where is God, then? Where is He when you need Him?"

"It doesn't work like that," I said. "He isn't Santa Claus, handing out presents."

"Then what's He good for, anyway?"

I held my tongue. This would only get worse, and I didn't feel like arguing with him when he was like this. I'd seen this with Mom. He'd just get louder and louder, and then he'd start yelling. And if we were home, he'd start throwing things.

"What are you doin' here?" I asked instead.

"Whatcha mean? It's a free country."

"Sure it is. But why are you here?"

"You mean right here, right in this spot?"

"Yeah, right here, in front of our house."

"Just passin' the time o' day," he said, grinning. "Havin' a few cold ones, watchin' the world go by."

"Dad, you're spying on us. Why?" I asked, feeling my stomach muscles tighten, just like they always did during really tense points in my tennis matches.

"I ain't spyin' on you, boy," he growled. "I'm your father, and don't you forget that. I can come and go as I please, and you do as I tell you. Don't you forget it."

"There's no way I'm gonna do what you tell me. Not now. Not after what you did," I said defiantly.

He reached across the car seat and tried to grab my arm. I jerked back in the nick of time, just escaping him. Even in his present state, he was still surprisingly quick.

"You'll do as I say, boy," he said, as he settled back in behind the wheel. "I promise you that. You'll mind me, or you'll mind my belt."

"No, I won't," I vowed. "Not ever."

He started the car. It roared into life, the muffler still shot. You could probably hear the car for miles around. "You won't be so smart next time, boy, when I give you a coupla good ones across the backside," he said, giving me his most menacing glare.

I stepped back from the car and didn't answer. I wasn't sure there was anything left to say.

"You wait," he said, jabbing a finger at me. "You'll see."

"I hope not," I said to no one in particular as the car roared away, knowing full well that there would almost certainly be another run-in with my father. There was just no escaping it.

**I'm not sure whose idea it was.** Probably Chris'. He's always dreaming up weird stuff to do, especially when he's bored.

He waited until Mom had left for work before springing it on Aunt Franny, of course. Mom would have said no, or at least put up a whale of a fight. But Aunt Franny was a pushover.

"No," Aunt Franny said immediately, when we presented the idea to her. "Absolutely not. Your mother wouldn't allow it, so neither will I."

"Oh, come on, Aunt Franny!" Chris said with the saddest, droopiest face he could muster. "Sure she would."

"Never," Aunt Franny said through tightly pursed lips as she held onto Timmy. "It's much too dangerous."

"Dangerous!" Jana blurted. "We've done stuff like this a billion times."

"That many times?" asked Aunt Franny.

"Sure," Jana said. "We always go out on adventures like this."

"Name the last time your mother let you do something like this," Aunt Franny said, trying to be reasonable.

Instinctively, we all turned toward John. But he really wasn't much help in this kind of situation. He'd remember certain facts, but then miss the whole picture.

"We've never done anything like this before," John stated flatly.

Jana and Chris groaned, but I decided to persist. "Now, John, I know we've never done anything *exactly* like this before, but can't you remember times when we've done different parts of it?"

"Like what?" John asked.

"Like riding our bikes?"

"Sure, we've ridden our bikes lots of times," he said.

"But never to the Vienna Metro station," Aunt Franny frowned. "That's a good four or five miles from here."

"Yes, that's right," nodded John. "Never to the subway."

"Wait," I said, holding up a hand and scowling at Chris to keep him from punching John in the arm. "I know we've never ridden our bikes to the Metro, but we've ridden them to places just as far away this summer. Right, John?"

"Yes, that's right," he nodded. "We've taken two trips out the bike trail, three trips to the movie theaters at the mall, and one trip on back roads to Clifton."

"That trip to Clifton and back was farther than the trip to the Metro," I said to Aunt Franny. "And Mom let us do that."

"Yeah, and the trip on the bike trail was a lot farther," Chris added.

Aunt Franny clearly was not sold on the idea. "But

you've never ridden on the Metro by yourselves?"

"I have," I said. "Karen has too."

"Karen isn't going," Jana said quietly.

"Why not?" I said.

"She said it sounds stupid," Jana replied. "She said it was kid stuff and she has better things to do."

I bit my lip. She was probably plotting some new rendezvous with our father, but now wasn't the time to get into *that* mess. We were a long way from convincing Aunt Franny, and it would take everything we had to get her to say yes. There was no time for diversions.

"Okay, well, I have, then," I said quickly, looking back at Aunt Franny. "It isn't hard. We all buy round-trip tickets to Washington and keep them in our pockets. We stay together in one car and get off at the right stop—"

"Foggy Bottom," Chris said quickly. "It's right before the Smithsonian. I looked it up on the map."

Aunt Franny almost smiled. It was hard not to in the face of such enthusiasm. "I see," she said.

"Then we'd surprise Mom at the State Department," Susan chimed in.

"I'm sure she'd love that," Aunt Franny said dryly, bobbing her head to one side to keep Timmy from grabbing her nose. "Why don't we call your mother first?"

"But then she'd know. It wouldn't be a surprise," Susan said.

We all held our breath. Aunt Franny glanced from one face to another, trying to read us. "Why do I get the feeling I'm up against five little con artists?" she asked.

"We are not," Chris said indignantly. I almost laughed. Chris was always pulling some kind of a scam. He was a world champion con artist if I ever saw one.

"Will you call me when you get to the Metro, and then when you get to Foggy Bottom and the State Department?" Aunt Franny said at last.

"Yes!" Chris and I said at the same time.

"And you'll walk your bikes across the busy streets?"

"We always do," Chris said.

"I doubt that," Aunt Franny said. "But will you do it, for me, this one time?"

"We will," Chris said. "I promise."

Aunt Franny looked at me sternly. "And you'll always keep both eyes on Susan and John?" I just nodded solemnly. Aunt Franny turned to Chris and Jana. "The two of you will stick together like glue and paper?" They both nodded solemnly.

Aunt Franny closed her eyes, and shook her head. "I can't believe I'm letting you do this," she said. "I really can't."

Chris held up two fists triumphantly. Susan tried to give John a high five. John missed her hand entirely and smacked Susan's shoulder. Jana just gave me a wink.

"Aunt Franny, it'll be all right," I said. "It's really pretty simple. I have the route all mapped out to the Metro, and the subway ride downtown is a breeze. After that, we'll be with Mom."

"Easy," Chris said. "No problem."

"Why don't you kids just let me drive you downtown to the State Department?" Aunt Franny persisted. "It would be a whole lot simpler—"

"No!" Chris groaned. "That would ruin it!"

"We just *have* to do this," Jana said. "How else will we ever learn about Washington? It's our home now."

Aunt Franny's guard was down, and Timmy finally managed to get through her defenses. He grabbed her nose and twisted, giggling the whole time. Aunt Franny managed to remove Timmy's hand, but he'd already moved to one of her ears by then.

"Okay, you can go," she said, sighing deeply. "But you had better be very careful. And I mean it."

"We will," I said with a confident smile. "Don't worry."

\* \* \* \* \*

We got lost, of course. I don't know whose fault it was. Probably Chris'. He kept going ahead of the rest of us, whizzing around corners and jumping curbs.

All I know is that somehow we wound up smack in the middle of a big university parking lot instead of Main Street in Fairfax, Virginia, and that I had to go inside one of the buildings and ask for directions to the subway.

One of the kids was nice enough to draw me a crude map on one of his notebook pages. I don't think we'd have made it otherwise—at least not before the sun went down. We took about a dozen turns before finally arriving at the Metro.

I locked all of our bikes together with a big chain lock, called Aunt Franny to tell her we'd arrived safely, bought all of the round-trip fare cards for everyone, and then made sure John didn't get stuck in the gate going into the place.

Once we'd arrived safely at the subway platform, I

still had my work cut out for me. Chris kept running up the down escalator, despite all the nasty glances he kept getting from passengers who were trying to make their way down the same escalator.

John kept wandering just a little too close to the railway tracks. I had to keep one eye on him, and one eye on Chris. That didn't leave any for Susan and Jana, so I made Susan hold her sister's hand. It was tough to get in trouble when you were holding some-one's hand.

The subway car finally pulled into the station. We piled aboard and settled into two of the seats at the rear of the car. Chris couldn't sit still. No sooner had the car left the station than he was up and wandering down the aisles.

It was just about then that it hit me. I tried to push the thought away, but it kept coming back.

I was sort of like their dad. It was silly and stupid and ridiculous and I really wished it wasn't so. But there was no denying it. If I didn't look out for them, there was no one else. Somebody had to pay attention right now, and I was the only possibility.

I wished Mom didn't have to work. I wished, with all my heart, she could be around all the time, like she had been before.

But she wasn't. And unless she got married again real soon—which wasn't likely—she wouldn't be around during the day. Which meant that we had to fend for ourselves every day until suppertime.

Oh, sure, Aunt Franny was always there. She was sort of like Mom. She always looked out for us, and did things for us. She was great.

But there were times—like now—when someone

had to pay *extra* attention. Just because. Usually it was your mom or dad. But our mom was working and Dad was probably still sleeping with the shades pulled down in his motel room somewhere.

"Chris!" I yelled. I was too late with my warning. Chris piled right into a couple that had stood up to leave at the next stop, and he took a hard fall against one of the plastic seats. He limped back toward us, favoring the leg that had smashed into a metal post.

"Why don't you slow down?" I asked him.

"Yeah, maybe I will," he said, wincing as he settled into the seat in front of me.

The rest of the subway ride was uneventful. Chris had quit bolting up and down the aisles, and we finally arrived at our stop intact. I hustled everyone off the train, and Chris was off to the races again. He at least waited at the top of the escalator for us.

I got my bearings from a map of the streets they displayed at the exit of the subway. The State Department wasn't very far away, and it only took us a couple of minutes to get there.

For a place that was supposed to run the world—or something like that—it sure looked dingy. Sort of beat up. I was expecting some kind of a palace. The place just looked like a huge, gray building with a whole bunch of rooms.

The guards paged our mom, and we had to wait in the lobby outside the metal detectors, the same kind they have at airports.

I heard Mom before I saw her. I heard the distinctive *clip, clip* of her black shoes as they came down the hallway. I could tell by the walk that she was hurrying.

I almost didn't recognize her. She looked so important—or something like that—with her State Department badge and her hair pulled back.

"Hi, Mom!" Susan yelled as she spotted her. Mom knelt down and gave her youngest daughter a big hug as she arrived in her arms.

Mom looked up, directly at me. Her eyes were smoldering. Somehow, I don't think she was enjoying this surprise much.

"Cally James, what's this all about?" she asked me in her sternest voice.

"It's a surprise," I said.

"It certainly is," she said, her voice controlled.

Boy, was she mad. I hadn't seen her like this since the day our father hit Susan with the back of his hand and Mom had stood up, right in his face, and told him never to do that again.

This was a different kind of mad, though. She was both worried and furious, all at the same time. She gave Susan another quick hug and stood up.

"Mom, we were *real* careful," I said.

"That's not the point," Mom said. "You know better than to pull a stunt like this."

"We didn't do anything wrong," Chris protested. "Aunt Franny said it was all right."

Mom frowned at me. "It's one thing to go down to the store, or even the mall. But to come all the way down here . . . "

"It wasn't all that hard, Mom," Jana said. "We only got lost once."

Mom's scowl deepened. "Just for a second," I said quickly, hoping still to avert a disaster. "We got right back on track."

"We wanted to see where you worked, that's all," Susan said. "We wanted to surprise you."

Mom looked down at Susan, and I could see the anger start to fade. I breathed a silent sigh of relief. Good, old Susan. Always there when you needed her.

"I called Aunt Franny from the Metro, to tell her we'd gotten there okay," I said, seizing the opening like I always did in a tennis match. "And I had the route all mapped out. It really wasn't all that tough."

"You still shouldn't have taken advantage of Aunt Franny like this," Mom said. "It isn't fair to her."

"We really did want to surprise you," I said softly. "We've never seen where you work, that's all."

Mom gave me a sudden smile. The storm had passed. She glanced at her watch. "All right, I give," she said. "It's almost lunchtime. I can take off for about an hour or so . . . "

"Can we see your office?" Jana asked.

"My office?" laughed Mom. "Well, sure, I guess, if you can call it that."

We all trooped through the metal detectors, down a long hallway, and through a foyer. Mom waved at a receptionist and turned into a very small room with no windows. There was a desk, a phone, a coatrack, and not much else in the room, except a big picture of us kids on her desk top. The six of us just barely fit into the room, it was so small.

"This is it?" Chris asked.

"This is it," Mom said. "Not much, but I'm not actually in here much. Usually, I'm wandering around the building with visitors."

"I'd go nuts if I had to stay in here much," Chris offered.

"I know," Mom said. "So would I." She exited her cubicle quickly and started to walk back down the hallway. "Let's go visit a couple of the museums," she called over one shoulder.

We all ran down the hall to catch up with her. It took a little bit to catch her. Mom walked pretty fast. I'd never really noticed before. But there seemed to be a lot of things I wasn't noticing these days.

"I think we'll hit the Air and Space Museum first," Mom said. "We can look at pictures of the moon, which is where I'll send all of you if you ever try anything like this again."

"Oh, Mom," Susan giggled. "You're funny."

"I know," Mom answered. "But I wasn't really kidding."

**9**

**Karen was fuming.** She was so mad she was literally hopping from one foot to another by the time we dragged through the door around dinnertime.

"I can't believe you guys went without me," she said bitterly as we all sort of collapsed on the couch and chairs in the living room.

I glanced over at Jana. This was her department. Jana just shrugged. She knew as well as anyone that there were times—and I guess this was one of them— that you just couldn't figure Karen.

"We asked you to go with us," I said finally.

"Yeah, but you didn't really tell me what you'd be doing," she said.

"Sure we did," Chris said.

"No you didn't," Karen said. "You just said something about riding your bikes somewhere. You didn't say you were going on some big-deal hike downtown to all these museums."

"Karen, don't you remember—"

"You *didn't* say," Karen said quickly, almost in tears. "You all just left without me. You probably didn't even want me to come with you."

"Karen, that's not true," I said. "Come on. You know we wanted you to come with us."

"Yeah, really, Karen," Chris added. "Just ask Jana."

"No," Karen persisted. "You didn't want me there. I just know it."

Actually, it *was* too bad Karen had missed the trip. One of the places Mom had taken us was the Smithsonian. And they had a special exhibit there, complete with pictures and everything.

It was the *real* story of Jesse James, our ancestor the outlaw. Not the legend that everybody hears about, but the actual history. It was a lot different than anything I'd ever heard of.

It turns out that Jesse James wasn't such a bad guy after all. Or, at least, he wasn't the terrible desperado the legends talk about. Actually, he seemed more like Robin Hood than anything else.

During the Civil War, Jesse James' family lived in the North, on the Union side. But Jesse liked the South, and joined a guerrilla band that fought the Union soldiers. As a guerrilla fighter, he was very courageous and brave.

After the war, Jesse James surrendered and went home. The only problem was that the enemies he'd made during the war wouldn't let him stay at home and had him declared an outlaw.

So, Jesse James ran away from home. For sixteen years, he refused to let himself be captured and punished for what he'd done during the Civil War. He kept himself alive by robbing banks and trains.

The governor of Missouri put up a reward for him and two members of his own gang killed him. They collected the reward, were sent to prison for murdering Jesse James, and then were pardoned by the governor.

What fascinated me was that Jesse James was probably not as bad as he seemed. If anything, it looked like he'd run away from home because he didn't have a choice, and then robbed all those banks and trains because he didn't know how to stay alive otherwise.

According to the history at the Smithsonian, Jesse James probably would have stopped being an outlaw and come back home if someone had let him. But no one ever let him, so he kept right on robbing banks and trains. And became an American legend.

At any rate, it was too bad Karen had missed the trip into town. She would have loved the exhibit. She'd probably have liked Jesse James. I know Jana thought it was pretty cool. Jesse was *just* the kind of boy Jana seemed to be attracted to.

And now, well, Karen was just spoiling for a fight. I felt sorry for Mom. I had a feeling that tonight wasn't going to be a whole lot of fun when she came home from work. Something was eating at Karen, making her miserable. And I could bet what was causing it all for her.

She'd probably seen Dad again, and Dad had put all these ghosts and goblins in her mind. He did that to you. He whispered about how crummy things were, how everybody was out to get you in the world, how the deck was stacked against you. And if you weren't careful, you could believe it.

Karen was believing it. She was listening to my father's babblings, paying close attention to what they had to say.

It was hard. Mom had once told me that the Bible talked a little about what happens to a family when someone in it chooses to follow Jesus Christ and someone else doesn't. It's like a war. Even brothers and sisters can become enemies.

I guess I understood it. Mom believed that this was God's world, and that we lived according to His rules. Dad seemed to make up the rules as he went along.

Somehow, those two didn't quite go together. You either believed in God or you didn't. Either there was a reason for things or there wasn't.

I felt like I was being forced to choose sides, between Mom and Dad. I didn't want to. I really and truly didn't. I just wanted Dad to stay away, to keep his anger and his fury to himself.

But he wasn't staying away. He was trying to draw Karen into the darkness with him, into the dark corners of his world where unseen demons whispered that everyone was out to get him.

I wished I could tell Karen to stay away, that she shouldn't listen to Dad. I knew it wouldn't do any good, though. Karen wouldn't listen to me right now. She wasn't listening to anybody, except Dad. There was no getting around that.

"Karen, I *promise* you that we really did want you to go with us," I tried one more time.

"You can say whatever you want," Karen said, her lower lip quivering slightly. "I don't believe you."

"Just because Dad says . . . "

"You leave him out of this!" Karen burst out.

"But I was just going to say . . . "

"I know what you're going to say!" Karen yelled. "It's what you always say about Dad."

"Look, Karen, I didn't mean anything by it," I said soothingly.

Karen didn't want any part of that. "I know *exactly* what you meant," she said, her eyes flashing. "And you just leave Dad out of this." Then she whirled and stormed out of the room.

*Sure, leave Dad out of this,* I thought. How were we supposed to do that? We could all feel his angry presence lingering in the room in Karen's wake. There was no way to leave him out of this. For better or worse, our dad was starting to work his way back into the family.

\* \* \* \* \*

Karen didn't even bother to show up for dinner. She stayed up in her room. Every so often, I'd glance at her empty chair at the dinner table and shake my head.

Finally, Mom couldn't take it anymore. She'd had enough. "Put your plates in the sink when you're finished, please," she said curtly to the rest of us as she scooted her chair back from the table. She hadn't really touched her own dinner.

"Mom, I'll do the dishes," Jana said quickly.

"I'll help," I said.

Mom gave me a strange look. I never actually volunteer for manual labor. I don't know what came over me.

But Mom turned without a word and left the kitchen. We all listened as she walked up the stairs slowly, the fifth and ninth stairs creaking as they always did.

I looked over at Jana. She just shrugged. She really didn't seem to know what was going on with Karen any more than I did. That wasn't a real good sign, either.

"Cally, let's go play baseball," Chris said.

"Not right now," I said back.

"Why not?" he asked.

" 'Cause."

"Your loss," he said, needling me.

"No, it's one you won't have to suffer through." I wasn't really paying attention to Chris, though. I was listening as hard as I could to see if I could pick up the argument that I was sure was about to begin upstairs.

It didn't take long. Within minutes, we all heard this muffled yell from the top of the stairs.

"What'd she say?" Jana asked me.

"Something about not being fair," I said. "I couldn't really tell."

There was another angry yell, louder and more distinct this time. Actually, it was more of a shriek. "I can see Dad if I want to!" we all heard Karen yell. "You can't stop me."

The door to Karen's room opened and slammed a moment later. The door to the bathroom slammed about two seconds after that. Karen had clearly barricaded herself in the bathroom, one of her favorite tactics.

Mom stayed up in Karen's room for a long time, but her daughter refused to emerge from the bathroom. Karen would wait in there all night if she had to.

Finally, Mom gave up. She made one last pass, stopping by the bathroom door long enough to ask Karen to come out. My sister didn't even answer, and Mom didn't push it any further. We all heard her begin to come back down the stairs, more slowly this time.

"If *I* ever did that, I'd be grounded for a month," Chris grumbled.

"Do what?" John asked.

"Treat Mom like that," Chris said.

"Like what?" John persisted. "Karen and Mom always fight like that."

Good old John. It always tickled me to see the way he looked at the world. "I think Chris means that this fight was a little louder than usual," I said.

"I don't know," John said, shrugging. "They've had some pretty loud fights before."

"I've never seen Karen this angry," Jana said quietly.

"Really?" I asked.

Jana's face was grim. "I'm not really sure what she might do next. Could be just about anything."

Mom came back into the kitchen, then, and we all stopped talking. Mom looked like she'd just seen a ghost. "I think we all should try to be extra nice to Karen for a while," she said softly. "Can we do that?"

"Sure," I said.

"No problem, Mom," Chris added.

All the other kids nodded. Mom looked at each of us. That's when I noticed the deep, dark-blue bags under Mom's eyes. Funny how I hadn't really noticed them before.

Jana was squirming in her seat. She was clearly struggling. "What's Karen mean about Dad?" she finally blurted out.

Mom sighed. "She wants to go stay with your father for a while."

"But I thought Dad was living in some crummy motel room?" I said.

"He is," Mom said. "That's why I said no to Karen. It isn't a proper home for her, and she knows it."

Now it started to make sense. Dad was really working on Karen, trying to pry her away. And once he had

Karen, then he sort of had something to bargain with. It made sense.

And it made me mad all over again. What Dad was trying to do was really lousy. Why didn't he just come to the front door and knock? Why did he have to be so sneaky about everything?

The door to the upstairs bathroom opened. We all hushed. Karen didn't come downstairs, though. I wish she had. We could have talked it out.

Instead, she went back into her room and closed the door, more quietly this time.

"I'm going upstairs to talk to her," Jana said.

"That would be nice," Mom said to her.

"I don't know what I can say to her, though," Jana said. "She's pretty stubborn."

"I know," Mom said. "Just be her friend. She needs one of those right now."

I turned to Chris as Jana left. "I'm up first," I said.

"No way," he countered immediately. "You were up first last time."

"I was not," I said. "Remember? You hit that home run your first at-bat."

"That was the time before," Chris said.

I sighed. "Okay, flip for it."

Chris jammed a hand in one of his pockets and tossed the coin in the air, caught it in his other hand, and stuck it on his arm. "Call it."

"Heads," I said.

Chris took a peek under his hand. "Tails. You lose."

"Let me see that," I insisted.

Chris bolted from his chair, toward the back of the house. "It was tails. I'm up first," he called over one shoulder.

"Not until I see that coin," I yelled after him.

I heard a *plink* in front of me. A penny rolled around on the floor. "All yours," Chris said. "I'll get the bat. You get the balls and the mitt."

I just shook my head and began to walk more slowly. Even when Chris lost he somehow managed to find a way to win.

As I walked outside, I instinctively glanced up at Karen's room. The light was on, and I could just barely see Jana leaning up against the wall. It wouldn't do any good, I thought. Karen *was* stubborn. Once she'd made up her mind, it usually took fifty-seven gorillas to wrestle her away from it.

A ball whizzed by my head, missing it by inches. "Pitch," Chris commanded. The mitt landed near my feet. Chris was waiting for me at the plate.

I scooped up the ball and mitt, took my place at the "mound" we'd set up in the backyard and went into my windup. Chris had to fall flat on his back to get out of the way of the first pitch, which I sent screaming toward his own head.

"The game has begun," I said with a vicious smile.

# 10

**An uneasy peace settled on the James house.**
For the next three days, we all walked around Karen
gingerly, as if she had some kind of a terrible disease
no one wanted to talk about.

Karen didn't make it easy. She just glared at me
whenever I tried to talk to her. So I stopped trying to
strike up a conversation. I was getting her message,
loud and clear.

I was the enemy. Dad had convinced Karen that I
had squarely joined forces with Mom. It seemed funny
to me, that a family could go to war against each
other. It was silly, in a way, and sad. It really
shouldn't be this way.

But Karen was convinced that Mom and I had
ganged up on her, that we were keeping her from
uniting the family as it had once been. She just
couldn't believe that it would never be like it had
been.

But Dad had ended that once and for all.

Meanwhile, though, I had something else on my
mind. Elaine Cimons had finally called, just as she'd
promised. We were going to study the Book of James
in the New Testament. The first meeting was at her
house Friday night.

"I thought it'd be fun for you, studying James," Elaine had said when she called.

"You picked that because of me?"

"Sure. Why not? Have you studied it much?"

"I, um, I've never read it."

"Great! Then this will be fun for you."

"Yeah, it'll be great," I said unenthusiastically.

"My house at 7 on Friday? Okay?"

"Sure, I'll be there," I said glumly.

"Do you think you can read the first chapter before then?"

"I guess."

"Okay, great, see you then, Cally."

I looked at the Letter of James that night. It's right after the Book of Hebrews, and just before the First Letter of Peter.

As always, whenever I opened the Bible, I was immediately drawn to the power of the words. They really lifted me right out of the world and into another place altogether.

The very first sentence of James hit me right between the eyes. It said that it was a good thing, a joyful thing, to go through trials and trouble because it made you steadfast. It perfected you, made you a better person.

"Count it all joy, my brethren, when you meet various trials, for you know that the testing of your faith produces steadfastness. And let steadfastness have its full effect, that you may be perfect and complete, lacking nothing."

That was very interesting to me. It seemed to mean that you should be happy when your father comes along and starts to tear away at your family, because in the end it would make those who made it through the test better, stronger people.

Well, that was surely true with Mom. She had seemed to grow in the face of adversity, not shrink away from it. She had faced up to the challenge, not run away from it. Steadfastness was having its full effect on my mom.

I showed up at Elaine's house about a half an hour before I was supposed to. But there was no way I was going in early, so I rode my bike around the corner and sat under a tree until 7.

I was so nervous I could hardly stand it. This was a whole lot harder than a big tennis match. With tennis, I could get past my nerves by whacking away at a few serves beforehand.

But I didn't have a racket in my hands here. There was no way to warm up for this. I just had to walk in cold.

Right at 7, I climbed back on my bike and rode back to Elaine's house. I met another boy just as he arrived on his bike, which he pitched on the lawn.

"Hi, I'm Barry Grimes," he called out.

"Cally James," I said, grim-faced.

We both made our way to the door. Barry was a few inches shorter than I was, with short-cropped brown hair, a face full of freckles, and clothes that didn't match and didn't fit. I guess he didn't pay much attention to the way he looked.

There were two other kids in Elaine's living room, a girl and a boy. Elaine introduced everybody as we got started.

Besides Elaine, I'd never seen any of these kids at Roosevelt. But the school was a big place, and it was easy not to know lots of the kids.

The girl, Sheryl Thompson, was sitting in the only chair in the room, probably because she was, well, really large. She wore a very loose-fitting dress, which hid it pretty well. But I could see that she was obviously very self-conscious about her weight.

The other boy in the room, Jason Pittman, wore round wire-rimmed glasses with hair cut so close it was almost a buzz. The top button on his shirt was fastened. His pants were creased and his shoes looked like they'd just been polished.

"Let's get started," Elaine said.

"Can I say something first?" Sheryl asked.

"Sure," Elaine said.

"Do we have to study the Book of James? Can we still do something else, like maybe the Book of Ruth in the Old Testament?"

Elaine smiled. I couldn't help it. I really liked it when she smiled. It made you feel good. "We can study whatever the group wants," Elaine said. "I just thought James would be fun, that's all. It's an important book."

"I know it is," Sheryl said quickly. "It's just that I thought it might be interesting to study a book named after a woman, for a change."

Elaine looked around the room at the three boys there. She was in a tough spot now, I thought. We hadn't even gotten started and we were already fighting.

"Well, I'll vote for the Book of James, in honor of Cally, who's coming to a Bible study for the first time," Elaine said firmly.

"I vote for Ruth," Sheryl said.

"All those in favor of studying James, raise your hand," Elaine said. Barry and Jason raised theirs. I kept mine in my lap. "For Ruth?" Sheryl raised hers again. I kept mine in my lap, still.

"You have to vote, Cally," Elaine said.

"I . . . I sort of thought I'd see what everybody else wanted first," I said.

Elaine frowned slightly. "Well, I guess it doesn't matter," she said lightly. "The majority is for James anyway . . . "

"But what would your vote be?" Sheryl asked, looking at me directly.

"Whatever the group wants, that's what I'm for," I answered evasively.

"But if you had to pick, which one would it be?"

"Either one would be okay," I shrugged.

Sheryl Thompson just glared at me. It wasn't much of an answer, and it certainly didn't seem to satisfy her. But that's how I felt. Actually, there was no way that I was going to give my real answer, which was that I didn't even want to be here in the first place.

"Okay, it's settled," Elaine said, opening her Bible.

"Can we at least study the Book of Ruth next?" Sheryl persisted.

"Why don't we see if we can just get through James first?" Elaine said.

"But if we do, and there's still time this summer, can we study Ruth?" Sheryl said.

Instead of growing angry or annoyed, as I was, Elaine suddenly reached over with this absolutely radiant smile on her face and gave Sheryl a quick hug. "Sure, we can study Ruth next," Elaine said. "That's a great book too."

Boy, that Elaine had something special. She was sure pushy, but she had something inside her that just brought people together.

"Can we start now?" Jason asked. He already had his Bible open, with a notebook and pen ready. I could see that he'd brought some notes with him, maybe two pages of them.

I glanced over at Barry. His Bible was open too. He'd crammed all these notes into the margin of his Bible, and he'd drawn boxes and circles around some of the passages.

I opened my own Bible. I had no notes, and I hadn't marked up any passages. Actually, I was having a little trouble remembering what I'd read in the first chapter. But it would come back to me. It always did, once I got to talking. I just needed a little prodding.

"What did everyone think of 19 and 20?" Barry asked suddenly.

I glanced down at my Bible. That was the passage about how a man should be quick to hear, but slow to speak and slow to anger. I laughed to myself. I always seemed to get that backwards. I'd get angry and yell a lot, and then I'd calm down and listen. Oh well.

"Shouldn't we start at the beginning?" Jason asked.

Elaine sighed. But she turned her own page back to the beginning. "Yes, we *should* start at the beginning."

I glanced around the room again, wondering how I'd gotten myself into this. It was going to be a very long night.

# 11

**Karen and Mom had the monster fight** I'd been waiting for that Saturday, in the sweltering, stifling heat of August. The heat can be unbearable in Washington during August. It can make you crazy.

The fight was bound to happen. Mom had managed to avoid Karen during the week. She would come home from work, keep her distance from Karen during dinner, and then watch as Karen drifted off her own way during the evening.

But Mom couldn't avoid Karen that Saturday, when the two of them usually helped each other out around the house. Under normal circumstances, Saturdays were fun for both of them. They joked around as they did things together.

But not now. They were like two weary prizefighters trapped on the canvas, ropes walling them in on all sides. They circled and circled, never really coming in for the clinch or the final knockout blow.

It really was a nasty day, with the temperature in the 90s and the humidity somewhere between soggy and drenching. I'd soaked three shirts by lunchtime.

I don't even remember what started the fight. Probably something dumb, like whether we should have ravioli or hot dogs for lunch. Or perhaps it began when

Mom asked Karen about her plans for that night, and Karen decided it was none of her business.

I guess it doesn't matter. Karen was itching for a fight. I'd seen it in her eyes for days. Jana had seen it coming too, but she felt as helpless as I did. Neither of us could stop Karen. She was bound and determined to reunite the family, whatever the cost.

We were out in back playing a game of tree-tag when the fight erupted. John was "It" again, as usual. As soon as Susan was tagged, she'd always wait until John tried to run from one tree to the next, and then she'd track him down like an experienced game hunter. Then John would try to catch someone until Chris or I slowed enough to let him get one of us.

John was in the middle of the yard, his hands planted on both hips, surveying the yard to see who he could catch, when the first shriek came hurtling out of the house.

"You can't tell me what to do!" Karen yelled at the top of her lungs.

We couldn't hear the reply, so I knew that Mom was still trying to keep it under control. Fat chance. Karen wanted nothing of that.

"No!" came a second shriek by Karen. "Dad would *never* make me do that!"

"But your father isn't here," we all heard Mom answer back, her voice a decibel louder.

"Because *you* won't let him come back!"

"Karen!" Mom said sharply. "I've had enough of that. It was your father's choice to leave this family, not mine—"

"But he's *changed,*" Karen said, still yelling. We couldn't hear Mom's answer. Whatever it was, it infuriated Karen. "He has changed," she said again. "You just won't believe it."

A few seconds later, we all heard a door slam. Then it slammed again, and again. Karen hadn't used that tactic—repeated door slams—for years. She was really mad now.

An uneasy silence settled on the house. John was still in the middle of the yard. The rest of us were standing with our hands resting on a tree, listening intently for some new sound to emerge.

Mom walked out of the back door. She walked over to me, her face a grim mask that hid the seething emotions I knew were raging just beneath the surface.

She handed me a ten-dollar bill. "Can you take the kids up to the store for some ice cream, Cally?" she asked me quietly.

"Sure, Mom," I said, nodding. "Whatever you want."

"Thank you," she said, pressing the bill into my hand and turning to walk back into the house. Her shoulders sagged and there was a kind of aching tiredness to her walk. I wanted to help so badly it hurt to think about it. But there was nothing I, or anyone else, could do right now. This was between Karen and Mom.

"Let's go, dudes," I yelled. "Ice cream, on the house." I waved the bill around so they could all see it.

"Yes!" Chris said. "I want chocolate fudge, with nuts."

"Ooooh, gross," Susan said, wrinkling up her nose.

"No way, it's the best," Chris said, as he and all the other kids started to congregate around me. I wondered if Mom wanted me to take Timmy too. But he was taking his morning nap, so it was probably better not to wake him up. He'd just have to sleep through the fight.

We heard a door slam twice more before we were out of earshot. I glanced over at Jana as we walked along the side of the road toward the convenience store that was about three blocks from the house. She just shook her head. She didn't know what to make of all of this, either.

As we walked, I began to think about how all of this might end. I'd never really thought about it before, for some reason. Perhaps because I didn't want to. But this had to end, somehow. Karen couldn't just stay mad for the rest of her life. Could she?

* * * * *

Susan and John were a mess by the time we got back. John had dribbled ice cream all down his shirt, and Susan's face looked like someone had spray-painted it.

Chris, of course, had managed to slurp down two cones, one right after the other. Which promptly sent him right to the moon. Chocolate and sugar have always done that to him, ever since he was real little.

Jana and I could barely eat our cones, though. Neither of us said anything about it, but we both had this crummy feeling in our stomachs that made it really hard to eat ice cream, or anything else for that matter.

The house was strangely silent, though, when we returned. Mom was sitting at the kitchen table, just staring out a window. She didn't even look at us as we all trooped through the kitchen. And Karen was nowhere to be found, at least as far as I could see.

"Mom?" I asked timidly.

Mom looked up. She'd been crying. Her eyes were blood red, and the dark-blue circles under her eyes seemed deeper than they ever had before. She didn't say anything to me right away.

"Is everything all right?" Jana asked.

"No," Mom said, her voice barely more than a whisper.

"Where's Karen," I asked.

"Gone," Mom said.

"Gone?" I asked.

"She just left," Mom said, her voice cracking a little. "She just ran out the front door and ran up the street."

"But where'd she go?" Jana asked.

"I don't know," Mom said. "She didn't say."

"But shouldn't you know? Shouldn't you find out?" Chris said impatiently.

I almost reached out and slugged my brother. Sometimes, he could be so . . . so unbelievably dumb. He just plowed right into things, without looking. And this was one of those times.

"And how am I supposed to do that, Chris?" Mom asked, not hiding the bitterness in her voice. "I can't force Karen to do something she doesn't want to, or tell me something she doesn't want to—"

"Sure you could," Chris said quickly. "You could send her to her room for about a zillion years."

This time, I reached out and slugged him. Hard. He'd probably have a bruise for a little while.

"Hey!" Chris said, grabbing his arm. "That hurt like crazy. Why'd you do that?"

"Because," I said, glowering at him.

" 'Cause why?"

"Because you're an idiot sometimes, that's why."

"But I didn't *do* anything, for cryin' out loud."

"Sure you did," I said darkly. "You were givin' Mom a hard time about Karen, and you don't have any idea what you're talkin' about."

"But I just said—"

"I know what you said," I answered sharply. "And I'm tellin' you to keep your big, fat nose out of it. This is between Mom and Karen, and they'll get it all straightened out."

Mom looked directly at me, then. Her eyes were brimming with sadness and regret. "Cally, I'm not so sure we will. I think we've lost Karen, for good."

"Oh, Mom, come on," I said, scowling. "That's just crazy. Where will she go?"

"Back to your father," Mom said.

# 12

**I couldn't sleep.** I rolled back and forth, either staring out the window at the few stars that peeked through, or at the dark corners of the loft where Chris and I both slept.

I just kept going over and over things, trying to figure a way out of the box that was suffocating our family. But there just didn't seem to be any way out.

I kept thinking about the Ten Commandments. "Honor your father and your mother," God told Moses. It was right there in the Book of Exodus. There was no mistaking what God meant.

But was I dishonoring my dad, when I thought about what a crumb-bum he was, and when I wished that he would just go away and leave us all alone? Was I dishonoring him when I wished with all my might that he would just let us be a family again?

I didn't have an answer. So I just kept tossing and turning, rolling the question around in my mind like a loose cannonball careening wildly around the deck of a ship.

It was probably about 3 o'clock in the morning when I heard the sound through my open window—the low, grumbling roar of the rusted-out Buick moving along the street in front of our house. There was no mistaking that sound. I'd know it anywhere.

I slipped out of bed and peered out a corner of the window that faced the street. A car was creeping up the street. Its headlights were off, but the sidelights were on, which probably gave him just enough light to see the road immediately in front of him.

Boy, Dad sure was being sneakier than usual tonight. Why didn't he just pull up, drop Karen off in front of the house, and roar away? Why was he being so secretive.

The car pulled up in front of the house. The engine cut off. I heard the slight creak of a door opening slowly, and an instant later a dark form moved quickly from the car and up the sidewalk leading to our house.

I turned away from the window and walked over to the doorway, listening intently. I heard the front door open slowly, and then I spotted Karen's dim shape as it moved up the stairway to her bedroom, which was actually a half-floor below our loft.

"What's up?" Chris hissed from the bunk bed.

"Nothing," I hissed back. "Go back to sleep."

"But what're you doing?" he said, still half asleep.

"Watching Karen."

"She's back?"

"Yeah, now go back to sleep."

"Okay," Chris mumbled. He turned over and pulled the covers over his head.

I could just barely see the door to Karen's room from my present vantage point. She didn't turn the light on, so I figured she probably just slipped right into bed.

I went back to the window and looked out. Dad's car was still there. He was out there, waiting. But what was he waiting for? Why hadn't he left?

When the answer came to me, I almost bolted from the room. But I thought better of it at the last moment. *No,* I thought, *better not to cause a scene. I'll just go see Karen in her room and try to talk her out of it.*

I slipped down the stairs from our loft as quietly as I could, making sure I didn't step on the stairs that creaked. I glided down the hall to Karen's room, and hovered outside the door for a second.

I could hear voices from within. Karen and Jana were arguing, fiercely, in hushed whispers.

"But you just can't!" I heard Jana say.

"I'm going," Karen answered back. "Dad needs me."

"But what about Mom?"

"I don't care what she says," Karen hissed.

Jana didn't answer right away. Then I heard tiny, muffled sobs coming from the room, so I figured Jana had started to cry. I eased the door open slowly and peered in.

Karen was sitting on the side of Jana's bed. She was crying on Jana's shoulder. Jana was holding her tightly, crying as well.

They both looked up at me as I entered the room, but I couldn't see the expressions on their faces in the darkness.

"Get out of my room, Cally," Karen said.

I stepped back into the doorway quickly, not wanting to upset Karen right now. "This better?" I whispered back.

"Why don't you just leave?" she said.

"Isn't that what you're about to do?"

"None of your business what I'm about to do," Karen said.

"But isn't Dad's car sitting out front, waiting for you?" I persisted.

"So what if it is?"

I took a tentative step into the room. Karen didn't say anything, so I took another. "Karen, this'll really hurt Mom a lot," I said softly.

"So what? She's hurt me a lot too."

"How? How has Mom hurt you? What's she done?"

"She . . . she just has."

"But how?"

"She won't even *try* to get back together with Dad," Karen said. "She won't even listen to me."

"Come on, Karen," I said, shaking my head. "Dad's the one who ran out on the family, not Mom—"

"But Dad's changed," Karen interrupted. "And Mom won't even talk to him, to see that he's changed."

"Well, maybe he has," I said slowly. "But you aren't going to solve all of this by running away with him."

"I'm not running away."

"Then what do you call this, sneaking off in the middle of the night without telling anyone?"

"I'm just getting some clothes," Karen said. "I'm not sneaking off."

"Karen, it's about 3 in the morning."

"So?"

"Why don't you wait until the morning. Tell Dad to come back and pick you up, so you can tell Mom what you're doing?"

"No!" Karen hissed. "She wouldn't let me go."

"I'm sure Mom would let you go visit Dad for a while," I said easily, wondering if that were really true.

Karen hesitated, mulling it over. But I already knew

what her decision was. "I'm leaving now," she said finally, rising from the bed. "And don't try to stop me, either of you. Just tell Mom where I've gone. Okay?"

I looked at Jana, who looked about as sad and forlorn as I'd ever seen her. She looked like her best friend in the world had just moved to the South Pole. Which wasn't all that far from the truth.

"I really wish you wouldn't go," Jana said.

"I have to, Jana, you know that," Karen said.

"I know, but I still wish you wouldn't do it," she said.

Karen opened the closet, pulled out a travel bag, and then began to open all of her dresser drawers and pull things out. She didn't lay them in the bag carefully. She just sort of threw everything in haphazardly. That wasn't like Karen at all.

She zipped the bag shut, glanced around the room one more time, and then moved over to the bed. She gave her sister a big hug. "See ya," Karen whispered in her ear.

She turned and walked toward me. I stepped farther into the room, and off to one side. Karen stopped, and gave me a hug too. I hate those, but I returned it.

"Come back soon," I said to her.

"We'll see," she said.

And then she was gone. I almost ran down the hall to wake Mom up, but I didn't. I don't know why I didn't. It was like I was paralyzed or something. I knew I should have told Mom, but it was like there was a big hand holding me in place. My legs just wouldn't move.

Jana and I stayed there like that, not moving, until we heard the roar of Dad's car a minute later. We both heard the gravel spray as he nearly laid a patch leaving the front of the house. We listened to the car as it sped away down the road.

"I'm gonna go tell Mom," Jana said finally.

"Yeah, I guess we should," I said. "I'll come too."

"Think we should have told Mom before Karen left?" she asked me as she got off the bed.

"Probably, but it's too late now."

"Guess it is," Jana said glumly.

As we walked down the hall toward Mom's room, our heads hanging low, I wondered again for about the billionth time why I always seemed to remember what the right thing was to do *after* the time I should have remembered it. Funny how it works that way. Real funny.

# ----⬤13

**I must have pounded about** a thousand balls into the net. I stood out there on the far court at the tennis club, blistering balls as they came screaming across the net at me.

I had the power on the automatic ball machine cranked up as high as I could, which meant that the balls were almost blurs as they came across the net at me.

I was taking the balls on the rise and whacking them back as hard as I could. After about an hour of this, my hands were almost bleeding. But I stayed out there, killing myself, because I wanted to get it right.

One ball after another cracked into the net just an inch or two below the tape. I just couldn't find the groove, that mystical place you need to find in sports that makes everything work out.

The balls just wouldn't rise enough to clear the net. I tried everything I could think of, but nothing worked. Every once in a while a ball would go over, but the next three would slam right back into the net.

It reminded me of my life right then. I was giving it everything I had, trying to live my life as I thought God wanted me to live it, and nothing seemed to work the way it ought to.

Mom was so upset about the way Karen had snuck away in the middle of the night that I thought she was never going to stop crying. It was terrible. I hated it when Mom cried. She just sort of sobbed quietly in her pillow in the bedroom.

*Phoomph!* sounded the machine, another ball coming at me. I stepped into it and cracked my backhand as hard as I could. *Whap!* the ball sounded as it slammed into the tape.

I'd felt so utterly helpless with Mom, so completely powerless to do or say anything that might help her. I'd wanted to hold her, maybe tell her that everything would be all right and that Karen would come home.

But I wasn't sure I believed it. Would Karen come home? Would my father ever let her? Or would he just cling to her, twisting her mind to suit his own evil designs? And was my dad truly evil, or was he just a poor, unfortunate soul who'd lost his way? Was Karen Dad's only hope?

As I always did when the going really got tough and I didn't know what else to do, I started to talk to God. It was the way I prayed. I didn't know if it was the *right* way, but I had a funny feeling there was no *wrong* way to talk to God. He'd listen no matter how you approached Him.

"God, you know how badly I can mess up sometimes. Well, this feels like one of those times," I thought, not really thinking much about the next ball as it came hurtling over the net at me.

"I know I'm supposed to honor my dad. I know that. It says it right in the Bible. It's one of the Ten Commandments. I wish with all my heart that I could do that.

"But, You see, I can't. I just can't. My dad is wrecking our family. He's destroying it. He's splitting it apart. It's hard enough for Mom without all of this. I don't know how she makes it.

"So what am I supposed to do? I don't want to hate my father. Is there some other way? Is there some way to make all of this work out? Can I love and honor my father, but still hate what it is he's doing to our family? Can I do that?"

Without thinking much, another ball came at me, and I hit it fluidly, gracefully, and it zipped across the net into the far corner. It was the third in a row I'd hit right, a small corner of my mind noticed. There was a tiny pool of balls gathering on the other side of the net now.

"Is that it, God? Can I hate the rotten, evil things my dad is doing but not hate my dad? Is that possible? Can I remember my dad the way Mom talks about him, when he was young, before he'd become so angry and cynical that he couldn't see straight anymore?"

I took another ball on the rise and crushed the return. It landed just inside the baseline, deep, in the far court.

"And can I go tell him that? Can I seek him out and try to tell Karen that she should come home until my dad gets things figured out? Would either of them listen to me?"

But I already knew the answer. I had to try. I didn't have a choice. I knew it was the right thing to do, no matter how it turned out. I had to go find my dad and Karen. I just had to.

I took five more balls. I sent each one of them

screaming back toward where they'd come from. My
hands were so raw that it would take a couple of days
to recover.

I didn't care. I had a funny feeling I wouldn't be
playing tennis for a few days. I would be out there,
somewhere, looking for my dad and Karen. How long
would it take? I couldn't say. But I wouldn't stop until
I'd found them. Of that I was now very, very sure.

# ⬤14

**I decided not to tell Mom what I had in mind.** At least, not yet. I'd try to find Dad first and see how it went.

Finding them, however, was going to be tough. I had no idea where Dad was staying. There were about a million hotels in Washington, and I couldn't just call every one of them.

I knew how Dad thought, though. He was real lazy, so he'd try to find a cheap place that was near an all-night convenience store, so he could buy his beer in the middle of the night. And he'd try to find some place that was near our house.

So, bright and early the next day and without telling anyone what I was doing, I set out on my bike and just started to cruise. I took a street map with me to make sure I covered every possible location within a couple of miles from my house.

After two hours, I was ready to give up. I hadn't seen a thing. In fact, I hadn't yet found a motel that was near a convenience store. The motels I did find were all run-down fleabags in the middle of nowhere.

I was staring at one of those run-down motels when it hit me. John could do this, and he wouldn't need a bike. He could do it with a map and a phone book.

"Boy, am I dumb," I muttered to myself, wondering now why I'd just spent two hours wandering around the neighborhood looking for motels.

I pedaled back home furiously. I ditched the bike in the front yard and raced through the front door.

"Where's John?" I asked Aunt Franny, who was in the kitchen with Timmy, fixing lunch for everyone.

I stopped dead in my tracks. Timmy, who was about to have his first birthday soon, had pulled everything he could lay his hands on into the middle of the kitchen. Every pot, pan, spoon, and spatula he could reach was piled on the floor of the kitchen. Aunt Franny looked like she was trapped against the stove.

"Something wrong?" Aunt Franny asked with an amused smile.

"It looks like World War III hit in here," I said.

"Timmy got a little carried away."

"A little?"

"He likes to help," Aunt Franny said.

We both looked at Timmy. He seemed so big to me. He'd been just a tiny baby only a few short months ago. Now, he was walking around, emptying kitchen cabinets. Soon he'd be talking.

And Dad had missed all that. He'd watched all the other kids grow up. But he'd only caught a glimpse of Timmy before he'd gone off the deep end and left the family. It suddenly occurred to me that Timmy wouldn't have the faintest idea who Dad was. Boy, was that strange.

For that matter, *Mom* had just barely seen Timmy grow up. Mom had always been home with the kids, had been with us every time we stumbled and fell, every time we couldn't handle something.

But now, she was off at work, trying to make ends meet. She only saw Timmy at the end of the day, when he was about ready to go to sleep, and on the weekends. It probably drove Mom nuts.

"Are you all right, Cally?" my aunt asked me.

"Yeah, sure," I said quickly, snapping out of it. "Just thinkin', that's all."

"About?"

"Oh, nothin', really. Just about how things have changed so much."

"Kids grow up fast," Aunt Franny said wistfully.

I glanced at my aunt, who'd never had kids. I'd never asked her why, mostly because it wasn't any of my business. Mom had once said something vague about an operation Aunt Franny had when she was real young.

"Aunt Franny, do you mind watching the kids during the day?" I asked.

"Of course not," she said, eyeing me curiously. "I love it. I was never able to have kids of my own, so this is about the next best thing."

"Really?"

"Really and truly," she said, smiling. "Now that your uncle has stopped wandering around Africa and the Middle East and settled down for a while, this is kind of nice. I love looking after you kids during the week."

"Uncle Teddy's been to places like that?" I asked.

"Cally James, you knew that," my aunt said, frowning.

I wrinkled up my nose. "I guess I did. I just sort of forgot."

My aunt sighed. I was always forgetting things like

that. I had a funny habit of not really paying attention to something until I had to. "John's out back, with Susan," Aunt Franny said.

"What?"

"John, your brother. You asked where he was."

"Oh, yeah, I forgot," I said sheepishly. "Thanks."

I hurried out of the kitchen before I could make more of a fool of myself. There was a loud *crash* just as I left. It sounded like Timmy had pulled the blender out from the lower cabinet.

\* \* \* \* \*

In order to get John to come inside and help with my project, I had to let Susan tag along. She asked about a zillion questions, none of which I answered. That only made her ask a zillion more.

"Why do you need to find this particular motel?" she asked.

"Just because," I answered as I set the phone book and the street map down on the round, marble coffee table in our living room.

"What's the phone book for?" she asked.

"To get the list of motels," I answered patiently.

"Oh. How do you know which motel you're lookin' for?" she asked.

"That's what I need John for."

"How can John help?" Susan asked.

I glared at my sister. There was no way to stop the questions. They never stopped. They only shifted directions, like a weather vane moves when a new wind blows from another direction.

"Susan, can you just let me explain this to John first?" I said, trying to keep the exasperation out of my voice. I think I failed.

John was sitting patiently on the couch, his hands folded in his lap. He was content just watching Susan and me talk. He always seemed to be content just watching. He liked to take everything in, and then process it. Heaven only knows where he stored all that information in his brain.

"Okay, John, here's the deal," I said. "I need to find a motel that's near a convenience store, like a Quick-Shop." Dad loved Quick-Shops the best. He said the beer was cheaper there.

"Why do you need to do that?" Susan asked.

"Because I do," I said, refusing to look at my sister.

"What do I do?" John asked, leaning forward.

I shoved the yellow phone book toward him. "Okay, first, scan the pages with all the motels on them."

"Under motels?" John asked.

"Yes, under motels," I said. It was strange, sometimes, the way John's mind worked. He could remember everything, yet he couldn't quite get from one thing to the next.

John opened the book and took about a minute to look at all the pages. "Okay, now what?" he asked, looking up.

"Look for the Quick-Shops, under convenience stores. Only the stores in Fairfax County."

John thumbed through the pages until he got to the "Cs." He looked at the pages for another minute or so. "Now what?" he asked me.

I frowned. It suddenly occurred to me that I hadn't quite figured this out myself. What did I ask John to look for?

"John, can you remember if there was a motel on the same street as a Quick-Shop?"

John thought about it for a second. I could almost see the synapses clicking in his brain. "Sure," he said after a few moments. "There are five of them together like that."

"What are the streets?"

"Arlington Boulevard, Lee Highway, Braddock Road, Route 28, and Wilson Boulevard."

I thought about it for a second. "Okay, Lee Highway, 28, and Wilson aren't around here, so we can throw those out," I said. "What are the addresses on Arlington?"

John closed his eyes. He had to think a second with numbers. They were a little harder. "5812 and 8617."

"That doesn't work," I said.

"Why not?" Susan asked.

"Because they're almost thirty blocks apart," I said.

"How do you know that?" Susan asked suspiciously.

"Because I do," I said, refusing to get drawn in.

"Okay, John, the addresses on Braddock?"

John went through his routine again. "7712 and 7715," he said.

"Yes!" I said, raising my hands in victory. "That's the place."

"What?" Susan asked.

"That's the motel I'm looking for," I said. "It's right across the street from the Quick-Shop. It's perfect."

"But how do you know?" Susan asked.

I ignored her for a second. "John, what's the name of the motel?"

"The White House Motel," he answered.

"I'll bet that's a real dump," I muttered. "Just like Dad, though."

"Is that where Dad's staying?" Susan asked.

"I think so," I sighed. "I don't know for sure."

"Are you gonna get Karen to come back?" Susan asked.

"I'll try, Sue," I said, looking straight at her. "I really will."

"But what if she won't come back? What'll you do then?"

"Beats me," I said. I stood up and gave John a friendly "whack" on the back. John just blinked furiously. "Thanks, John," I continued. "This was a big help."

Susan scrunched her face up and glowered at me. "You know, Cally, you could have done that yourself," she said. "It wasn't all that hard to look the addresses up."

"I know," I said, smiling. "But it was more fun watching John do it."

**The address John had found** for the White House Motel was about twelve blocks away, so I climbed back on my bike and raced to it. I don't know why I was in such a hurry. I just was.

The motel really was a run-down, moth-eaten flea-bag. Paint was peeling everywhere. The parking lot had all kinds of weeds growing up between the cracks. The pool in the front was covered with gunk and green algae.

I was so sure this was the place I didn't pull right into the parking lot. I hovered on the fringes, scanning the lot for the telltale Buick.

I think I stood there, staring at the few cars in the lot, for about five minutes. I just couldn't believe my father's car wasn't there. I was so *sure* this was the right place. I could feel it in my bones.

There really was a Quick-Shop right across the street, and I decided to go get a Slurpy and figure out what I was going to do next. I zipped across the street, leaned my bike up against the wall, and went in. The Slurpy machine was around the corner, partially hidden from the entrance.

I heard him before I saw him. "Hey, y'all," this voice boomed from the front of the store. "How's tricks?"

I almost spilled the lime-green ice I was pouring into my cup in my haste to set it down on the counter. I peered around the corner. My dad had just come into the store. He was alone. He was just passing by two elderly, Korean clerks when I spotted him. They were just staring at him.

When the two clerks didn't answer him, my father threw his head back and started to guffaw. "That so?" he said in between laughs, slapping a hand down hard on the counter. One of the clerks jumped a little. They probably thought my father was crazy.

As he made his way toward the back, where they kept the beer, the two clerks started jabbering away in Korean. I could have sworn I heard one of them say something about "911."

When I was sure my dad was at the back of the store, I left my half-filled Slurpy on the counter and bolted for the front door. I burst through without looking back, grabbed my bike, and raced out into the street. I was lucky. There were no cars on the street.

I ditched my bike next to the door that led into the motel office. There was nobody there, so I started to bang on the bell at the counter.

It took forever for someone to show up, but finally a huge woman with hair that looked like it hadn't been combed in months came sauntering slowly through another doorway.

"Whatcha need, kid?" she said, picking at her teeth.

"Is there a James staying here?" I asked politely.

"Jim what?" she asked through a mouthful of fingers.

"No," I said, barely able to control myself. "That's his last name."

She glanced down at a book on the desk behind the counter and then back up at me. "What's it to ya, kid?" she asked, eyeing me coyly now.

"Look, he's my dad," I said, starting to fidget. "Is there a Tom James here or not?"

"Maybe," she said nonchalantly. "You still haven't told me why you're askin'."

I glanced down at the book. I was pretty good at reading upside down. I always read stuff upside down at school just to kill time.

Halfway down the guest book, I spotted my dad's name. He was in room 7. I turned and almost ran out of the office without another word.

"Hey," the office lady yelled after me as I left. "Do you wanna know if he's here or not?"

I didn't answer. I ran down the sidewalk, glancing across the street to make sure the rusted-out Buick was still at the Quick-Shop. It was, so I figured I still had a few minutes.

Karen was sitting on the bed, just staring at the television. I didn't even bother to knock on the half-open door as I entered the room. Karen sort of jumped to one side as I careened into the room.

"Hey!" she exclaimed. "How'd you find us?"

I didn't say anything right away. I glanced around the room. It was an absolute pigsty. Dirty clothes and empty beer cans were strewn everywhere. I spotted three half-eaten pizzas resting on countertops. The place smelled like one of those restrooms at a football stadium.

Karen's bags were easy to spot. She hadn't really unpacked yet. Her bags were mostly full of clothes, sitting on the second, neatly made bed on the opposite side of the room. I started to walk across the room toward them.

"What are you doin'?" she asked, turning to face me.

"Getting your bags so we can go," I said.

"I'm not going anywhere," she said angrily, her eyes blazing.

"Karen, this is crazy. Look at this place. It's a mess. You can't stay here."

"We're only stayin' here for a little bit. That's why it's a mess."

"Yeah, sure," I said, reaching for her bags. "And where would you go?"

"Don't touch those!" she said sharply.

I stopped and turned back toward my sister. "Okay. So where are you goin'?"

"None of your business."

"Oh, come on, Karen. This is really dumb. Why don't you just come back with me? We can talk to Mom—"

"I don't have anything more to say to her," she said quickly. "I'm livin' with Dad now."

"In this slop?" I asked.

"Like I said," she pouted, "we're goin' back soon, and then it'll be better."

"Going back?"

Before Karen could answer, the door slammed open. My father came striding through, but then stopped dead in his tracks when he saw me. He threw the brown bag he was carrying onto the bed.

"Cally, boy, whatcha doin' here?" he said, cocking an eye toward me.

"Just talkin' to Karen," I said evasively.

"How'd you find me, boy?" he asked.

"John figured it out."

My father gave me a cockeyed grin. "Yeah, he's somethin', ain't he?"

I didn't answer. I glanced back at Karen, imploring her silently to come with me. She started to shake her head violently.

I'm sure my dad knew why I was there. It wasn't all that hard to figure out. "Why don't you just let Karen and me go back?" I said.

My father started to laugh. It was a guttural, humorless laugh that made me angry more than anything else. "Karen can come and go as she pleases. Right, kid?" Karen nodded. "See? So you go back and tell your mother there's no problem. Karen's stayin' with me for a while."

"Karen?" I said, turning back to my sister again. She just shook her head again, silent.

"Cally-boy, you tell your mother that it's gonna be different now and that I'll be waitin' for her. When she wants to find me, tell her she can find me in the fires of hell." He started to laugh demonically. "Except hell ain't there no more. The fire's gone." He started to laugh again at his own insane joke.

"Dad, I don't understand," I said.

"You just tell her what I said. Tell her that Karen's mine now, and that I'll be waitin' for her. Got it?"

A shiver went down my spine. I almost felt as if I didn't know my own father anymore. Who was this man who had changed so much in the past year? Where was my dad, who used to toss a football with me after his shift when I was a little kid?

"Dad, I don't think—"

"You just tell her!" my father said sharply, cutting

me off. "Now get, 'fore I take my belt to ya."

I looked at Karen one more time. She looked away. I started to leave the room, my head hanging low. I had failed so utterly, so miserably, that I felt like crawling home.

"You tell her, Cally," my father called out at me before slamming the door behind me. There was an ominous *click* as he locked the door. I had a funny feeling that we'd just entered a long, dark tunnel. And I had no idea where the light was at the end of it.

# 16

**"What?" Mom asked that night.** "He said what?"

I was having a very tough time explaining to Mom what I'd done, and an even tougher time trying to explain what it was Dad had meant about things being different and that he'd be waiting for her.

"That's what he said, that he'd be waiting. I don't know what it means," I said hopelessly. I left out the part about the fires of hell, because that didn't seem to make any sense at all.

"Was Karen all right?" Mom asked anxiously.

"Yeah, she seemed okay."

Mom started to pace the room. She almost never did that, so I knew she was really upset about all of this. I didn't think she was really mad at me or anything. She just hated what was happening to our family.

"Does he mean that he's waiting for me to come over to the motel and talk to him?" she said finally. "Is that what he means?"

I shrugged. "Maybe. But don't ask me. I don't have a clue."

"But if that's what he wants—just to talk—why doesn't he just bring Karen here? We can talk here."

"Mom, I really don't know. He just said that Karen was his now and that he'd be waiting."

Mom closed her eyes. "He makes it sound like he's kidnapped his own daughter."

"Well, he has, sort of," I said slowly. "I don't think Karen really knows what she's doing."

Mom stopped pacing and looked directly at me. She'd made up her mind. "Come with me? You could show me where he is."

"If you want me to, I will," I said.

"Let's go, then," she said, turning away to look for her purse and her car keys. "Let me just go tell Jana what we're doing, so she can look after the kids."

* * * * *

There weren't very many cars in the parking lot of the White House Motel when we pulled up. Not that you could see the parking lot all that well. All the lights surrounding the lot were either broken or burned out. Only the street light nearby illuminated the place.

Dad's car wasn't in front of his room, and the window to his room was dark. We got out of the car, and I walked over to the window and peered in cautiously. I couldn't see anything. It was too dark inside the room.

Mom knocked on the door. When no one answered right away, she knocked more loudly. I walked over and rapped on the door, hard.

"Anybody home?" I called out.

We waited for about a minute longer, and then turned to head toward the office. I didn't like the looks of this, not at all.

The same office lady—with the uncombed hair—was still there. She was eating a huge bag of french fries and washing them down with a beer. I wondered if she slept here too.

She started to get up as we came in, but sat right down again and kept eating when she recognized me. "You find your pop before, kid?" she asked in between mouthfuls.

"Yeah, I found him," I said. *No thanks to you,* I thought silently.

"Well, you were sure lucky, then," she said, tipping the beer to her mouth and guzzling it for a couple of seconds.

"What do you mean?" I asked.

"Nothin', 'cept he bolted outta here like his pants were on fire almost right after you stopped by," she said.

"You mean he checked out?" Mom asked. I could see her heart sinking right through the floorboards.

" 'Course he checked out," she said. "Paid his bill with all these lousy, crinkled-up ones too."

I looked at Mom sharply. Karen always kept money stashed in this huge sock at home. That was her bank. She just stuffed money in it, and hid it in her closet. None of us were supposed to know about it, but I'd known about it for years. I was sure Mom knew about it too.

"Did he say where he was going?" Mom asked, ignoring me for the moment.

"C'mon, lady. Waddya think I am, a travel agent or somethin'?"

"I just thought maybe he might have mentioned where he was going," Mom said easily, trying not to offend her.

"Look, see, as far as I'm concerned, as long as they pay their bills, what do I care about where they're goin' to? Ain't none o' my business."

My mom looked crushed. We were back to square one. "I see," she said. "Well, then, thank you for your time." Mom and I started to leave.

The office lady cleared her throat. It was a gurgling, croaking sound. " 'Course, that don't mean I didn't happen to overhear a bit o' their conversation," she said, cocking her head to one side.

"Whose conversation?" I asked sharply, turning back.

"Your pop, and that brat with him," she said.

"So what did they say?" I asked, trying to stay calm.

The lady leaned so far back in her chair I thought she was going to tip over backwards. That would certainly be interesting to watch, I thought. The chair creaked and groaned under the pressure.

"Well, lemme see," she said slowly. "I reckon I *might* be able to remember. But I might need a few more o' these to jog my memory a little." She held the half-empty beer up in front of her.

I could see the jaw muscles tightening on my mother's face. "How many of those?" she asked tightly.

"Oh, I dunno," she said. "Maybe a six-pack would do it."

Mom let out a careful, measured breath. She opened her purse. "Think a five would cover a six-pack?" she asked the lady. Mom placed the five on the counter.

The lady's meaty arm whisked the bill off the counter so fast I barely had time to blink. "Yeah, that'll cover it nicely," she said, stuffing the bill in her pocket.

"And?" Mom asked.

"Well, you know," she said slowly. "My memory's a

funny thing. Sometimes it takes a second six-pack to rev it up some."

Mom took a step toward the counter. "I think," she said softly, "that one six-pack is more than enough to jolt your memory."

The two of them stared at each other for a moment. The office lady blinked. "Yeah, well, mebbe you're right," she said. "I do seem to recollect what they said, now that you mention it."

"Well?" Mom asked.

"He told the brat to make sure she'd gone to the little girls' room, 'cause they weren't stoppin' for a while." The lady took another swig of beer. "The brat asked how long it took to get to Alabama, and he said it was none o' her business, to just sit tight and let him do the drivin'."

Mom looked over at me. There was clear panic in her eyes. Dad had taken Karen back to Birmingham. That's what he meant about waiting. He wasn't waiting for us here. He wanted Mom, and the whole family, to go back to Birmingham.

"Thank you," Mom said stiffly.

"Hey, thank *you*," the lady said, patting her pocket fondly. "Six-packs sure do help beat the heat."

As we left the office, I whispered, "It'll be all right. Really. Everything will work out."

"I don't know, Cally," she said, her voice tired and defeated. "There doesn't seem to be an end to this."

"We'll find it, you and me. Don't worry."

Mom laughed. It was nice to hear that. It meant she wasn't really letting all of this get to her. "All right, Cally, if you say so. But I'm going to hold you to that prediction."

# 17

**Good old Aunt Franny.** Since we'd moved to the Capital, she always seemed to be there when you needed her.

"Of course I'll look after the kids while you're gone," she said. "Don't you even worry about it."

"But Timmy—" Mom began.

"Timmy will be perfectly all right," Aunt Franny said, clasping my mom's hands. "He's used to me now. He'll be as happy as a lark."

"I'll help too," Jana chimed in.

"Thanks, honey," Mom said affectionately, giving her daughter a big hug.

"Yeah, and me too," Chris added.

"That's not worth much," I said, slugging Chris. He punched me back.

Mom glanced around the big family room at all of her kids, the Capital Crew she called us sometimes. Minus one. There were tears in the corners of her eyes. "You guys are great," she said, her voice a little raspy.

"We'll be fine," Jana said. "You just go bring Karen back. Okay?"

Mom nodded firmly. She blinked a couple of times to clear away the tears. "Okay, I will." She turned to me.

"Ready?" I nodded, and moved toward the door. I'd already stowed our bags in the back of the car.

And we were off. Everybody waved as we pulled out of the driveway. I couldn't help but remember when we'd driven into Washington for the first time. That seemed so long ago. Ages ago. So much had changed since then.

Mostly, I think, I had changed. Never mind that I'd won a national tennis championship. That didn't seem like all that much, really. It just sort of happened.

No, what had changed was that I'd gotten used to the fact that Dad wasn't around. I'd stopped worrying about whether there was going to be some big, hairy fight around the house after school.

I'd gotten used to a quiet, peaceful house, with Mom reading to Timmy at night, or Jana and Karen jabbering on softly about some boy at school, or Susan asking me to help her with her math.

I liked it that way. I was happy. I didn't want to go back to the way it was, always wondering when the next fight with my dad would happen. That wasn't any fun. It just wasn't.

\* \* \* \* \*

"So how long till we get there?" I asked Mom.

She smiled, and relaxed her death grip on the wheel of the car just a little. It had started to drizzle lightly, and Mom was peering hard out the window trying to see. She hated driving in the rain.

"172 hours," she said, keeping her eyes on the road.

"The way *you* drive, that's probably true," I countered.

"I'm a careful driver, that's all."

"Mom, even turtles stranded in the middle of the

road don't panic when they see you coming."

"That's not fair."

"Did you know that when you come to a stop sign, you actually stop, and then look back and forth about a hundred times before you finally go?"

"So what's wrong with coming to a full stop?"

"Nothing, but you don't have to put it in Park and wait for half an hour."

"Oh, quit exaggerating so much," she said in mock protest.

We both started laughing. Mom knew all too well that she was about as cautious as they come. She always drove the speed limit, she obeyed all the traffic signs, and she waited patiently for just about everybody on the road. It drove me absolutely nuts.

We'd just left the Beltway that surrounds Washington. We were driving south on the interstate, toward Richmond, Virginia. The traffic was terrible, which was pretty normal for Washington.

Mom had told me to pack enough clothes for myself for a week. I had no idea if that was really enough. I guessed time would tell. I had no idea, really, what was liable to happen in Birmingham.

One thing was certain, though. I was willing to stay down there until we'd pried Karen away. I didn't care what it took. Dad was not going to keep her as a hostage. I'd do anything to make sure of that.

\* \* \* \* \*

As we got closer to Birmingham, my stomach started to tighten up. Just like before a match. That's what it felt like.

You know, it was funny, but I was pretty sure Mom didn't have a plan. I know I didn't. I had absolutely no idea what to do, how to get Karen back.

We couldn't take her back. Dad wasn't about to just *give* her to us. And I knew Mom wasn't going to do what Dad wanted her to do, and move the family back in with him.

*So what can we do? Beats me. I guess we'll just have to take whatever comes at us.* It reminded me a little of a tennis match against an opponent I'd never seen. You just have to wait and see how the points play out, and then seize the advantage when you see it.

Right now, there didn't seem to be much of an advantage. Dad was the one who held the upper hand. It was strange, thinking of this as a competition, but that's the way I thought about it. The one thing I couldn't figure out was how you won or lost.

Maybe no one would win, though. Maybe we'd get to the end, or get to wherever it was we were going, and there would only be losers. That's what I couldn't figure out. I just couldn't sort any of it out.

"Where do you think he is, Cally?" Mom asked me when we were about fifteen miles outside of the city limits.

"I think he's gotta be near the mountain, probably near where we used to live," I said.

"I think so too," she said somberly. "But for the life of me I can't think of a place he'd stay that I'd think of right away."

I leaned back in my seat. Mom was right. Where would Dad stay, now that he had no job and no money? He'd probably used up everything he had just to get to Washington. That's why he probably "borrowed" the money from Karen's sock bank to pay the motel bill.

"At a friend's house?" I offered finally.

"I don't think he has any of those anymore," she said. "He ran most of those off."

"At another crummy motel?"

"Sure, but which one? How would we find him down here?"

"I guess you're right," I said, sighing.

"Was there anything else, Cally?" Mom said after awhile.

"Anything else?"

"Did Dad say anything else to you, besides that he'd be waiting?"

I wrinkled up my nose. "Yeah, well, there was this one thing. It didn't make any sense . . . "

"What?" Mom asked intently.

"It was nothin', really. Just that you could find him in the fires of hell, except that they weren't there anymore."

"The fires of hell?"

"Yeah, he said something like 'hell ain't there no more, the fire's gone.' " I shivered a little, remembering his laugh as he said it.

Mom stared at the road ahead for a while, thinking hard. She was hardly breathing. Then, suddenly, she relaxed her grip and settled back in her seat, a funny half-smile playing across her face.

"What? What is it?" I asked eagerly.

"I know where he is," she said softly.

"So are you gonna tell me or not?" I asked.

Mom didn't answer right away. "He's at the steel mill," she said finally. "That's where he is, in the bellows, where he used to work."

"The steel mill?"

"Sure," Mom said, smiling. "It's mothballed, and they probably don't even keep the dogs around the place anymore to protect it. And I'm pretty sure they haven't sold the land yet. Nobody wants the place."

"And the fires of hell?"

"The old forge, where they used to make the steel," she said. "He loved that place. He loved how hot it was, and that he could stand it. He used to walk around the edge, looking in. It gave him a feeling of power, to be able to stand right at the edge of that fire."

"Like the fires of hell," I said, shaking my head in amazement. I was sure Mom was right. It made a lot of sense that Dad had returned to the place where he'd been the king of the land.

Mom looked out through my side window. The sun was starting to set in the west. "I think we'll stop at a motel for the night, and go by the mill in the morning. I don't want to go by there at night."

"Me neither."

Mom pulled off a few minutes later and signed us up at the EZ Sleep Inn. But I doubted I'd get much sleep, not with images of fires and bellows and red-hot steel cascading through my mind. No, I didn't think I'd get much sleep at all.

# 18

**Boy, was I glad to see the sun.** I watched it come up over the horizon, not from the comfort and warmth of my bed, but from beside the highway outside our motel.

I'd actually fallen asleep almost when my head hit the pillow the night before. But I tossed and turned all night, images of my dad and Karen alternately drifting through my dreams.

I'd finally woken up just before dawn. When I couldn't fall asleep again, I'd gotten dressed and taken a walk outside. There wasn't much else to do, really.

Mom was already up too when I wandered back and knocked on the door between our two rooms. She'd already taken a shower and dressed. She gave me a tired smile when I came in through the door.

"Sleep well?" she asked.

"Not much," I said, shaking my head.

We didn't say much of anything to each other as we gathered up our things and took them to the car. I guess there wasn't a whole lot to talk about.

We didn't have a strategy, really. I don't think Mom knew how she was going to confront my father. More than likely, Dad had a proposal. I knew Mom wouldn't accept it. The question was what happened after that.

I stared out the window in silence as we drove the last ten miles or so to the old steel mill. As we got closer, I began to remember a few of the landmarks.

Once upon a time, before John and Susan were born, we only had one car. Mom used to pick Dad up after his shift. I still remembered sitting in the backseat of our car, listening to Karen and Jana jabber and fight with each other.

It had been a big, old car, a real gas-guzzler. The thing had seemed huge to me. I sometimes wondered how Mom was able to drive it without running into anything.

Sometimes Mom would stop off at a store on the way there and pick up candy bars for us. Never on the way back. If we stopped after we'd picked Dad up, it was usually just to buy beer, bread, and milk. Dad would leave the car running and go into the store himself. We all stayed behind and waited.

It was funny, but I could almost remember the smell of that car. It was a strange mixture of Mom's perfume and the slightly burned smell of Dad's clothes.

I bolted upright in my seat. *Wait a minute,* I thought, *hadn't that car been an awful lot like . . .*

"Mom?" I said.

"Yes, Cally?"

"That car, the one you used to pick Dad up in when I was younger, it was a Buick, like the one Dad has now, wasn't it?"

Mom thought about it for a second, and then nodded. "I think so. They look quite similar."

"I thought so," I said, resting my head against the window again. Another piece of the puzzle fell into place. Dad was trying to recapture something he'd lost. But he'd never be able to. Never. . . .

*   *   *   *   *

The rusted gates stood out starkly against the gray sky. The lock had been picked long ago, yet someone had swung the gates shut. Off in the distance, the colossal, dormant mill rose against the horizon, its long smokestacks jutting up like exclamation points.

I got out of the car and opened the gates to the mothballed steel mill. I flung the gates back and Mom drove through carefully. I climbed back in the car once it was inside the gates.

"Do you think he's really here?" I asked quietly.

Mom just nodded grimly. "Yes, I do."

"But isn't all this sort of crazy?"

She glanced over at me. I could see from the look in her eyes that she was just a little terrified right now. I didn't blame her. "Your dad's a little crazy inside right now, Cally. I don't think he's entirely sure of anything."

In Washington, especially around the Capitol and the White House, the bums, vagabonds, and the homeless always seemed to wander around in an endless trek to nowhere. I remember wanting just to avoid them when I saw them for the first time.

But, at the same time, I knew that those people could be anyone at all. Even my dad.

Mom had once shown me a verse in the Book of Revelation, about people who thought they had everything. Yet Jesus told them that they were "wretched, pitiable, poor, blind, and naked."

Dad had it all, once. A wonderful, loving family, a big house on a hill, and a job that seemed to stretch off into eternity. But that was all gone now, forgotten and fading.

As we drove deeper into the heart of the stone-cold mill, a peacefulness began to settle on my heart, easing the burden of the memories of something that would never be again. I was almost beginning to see the world, now, through my dad's own troubled eyes.

It was funny. By the time we'd arrived at the entrance to the mill, the transformation was almost complete. Somehow I understood him better.

For days, weeks, and months, I'd waited for just this moment. I'd waited for the day I could confront my father.

Yet, now that it was actually here, God had given me a new heart. I knew, now, how to honor my father — by loving him, unconditionally. There was no other way.

# ──19

**A shadow flitted across the door** to the great mill. We both heard the footsteps receding deep into the heart of the vast building. Mom glanced at me. I just shrugged.

If Dad was truly here—and both of us were now certain he was—then he sure was being mysterious about all of this. But maybe he felt like he had no choice. I just didn't know.

Mom stepped through the doorway first, and I followed close behind. We both stopped for a moment to let our eyes adjust to the dimness inside. The inside of the building was musty, and huge.

All the equipment had been moved out and sold off long ago. Just the shell of the place remained.

I glanced up towards the ceiling at a small crack in the roof. Dust particles danced around in the shaft of sunlight that tried to find its way down to the floor far, far below.

We both heard the *clink* off in the distance. It sounded like a wrench falling onto a metal floor.

"The big furnace room?" Mom asked me.

"Sounds like it," I answered. "Isn't it at the back of this building?"

"Yes, it is," Mom said. "Are you ready?"

I nodded. "As ready as I'll ever be."

"Let's go, then," Mom said. She reached out and took my hand. I didn't pull back. I gripped her hand hard as we started to walk toward the back of the mill. Mom's hand was ice-cold. She was absolutely scared to death.

"Mom, everything will be okay," I said. "You'll see."

She gave my hand an extra squeeze. "I know," she whispered. I think she was less scared than I was, actually.

There was a flickering light coming through the doorway of what had once been the furnace room. We walked toward that light quickly, and ducked through that doorway without a word.

We were both a little shocked at what we saw. I know I was.

Dad had arranged the room as sort of a palace hall. There was a long rug leading across the room to a sort of dais—a raised platform—and an overstuffed reclining chair. Actually, the rug was made up of a bunch of old pieces of different rugs, laid out end to end.

I recognized the sofa chair. It was the same one Dad used to sit in at home and watch TV from after his shift. He'd sink into that thing with a beer in one hand and watch for hours.

He was sitting in the chair now. Karen was standing beside it.

It was so strange, so alien, I almost wanted to turn around and walk away. I felt so very, very sorry for Dad.

Mom and I stood there, not moving a muscle, and looked around the room. There were other pieces of furniture strewn around the room in a haphazard fashion. Other than the long rug leading to the sofa chair on the dais, there was no rhyme or reason to anything in the room.

There was a mattress on the floor in the far corner of the room, a few bags piled next to it. Several feet away was an old, wooden table with a couple of chairs tucked under it. Dad must have straightened up a little before we came.

I spotted a cooler tucked against another wall. There were a few empty cans beside it.

Dad had strategically placed candles around the room, to illuminate the big furnace room. It still didn't light the place very well. It was hard to see everything.

Mom, still holding my hand, took a tentative step toward the dais. I followed with her. Neither of us had any idea what to expect.

Dad didn't say anything as we approached. He just watched us. The silence began to stretch out, an eerie companion to this room.

"Hi, Karen," I said finally, trying to push the shadows back to the corners.

"Hey, Cally," she said, her voice almost cracking. I looked at her, hard. She was standing ramrod straight next to Dad. I could just barely see her face, but it was clear to me she was terrified. I'm sure this place had scared her witless.

You see, Karen had always thought that Dad had just made a few mistakes along the way. That's all. She just thought he'd chosen unwisely and that he wanted to make amends now.

But Dad had gone over the edge. He hadn't just run away from the family. He'd run away from his own mind as well. It was clear to her now. I was sure of that. Our father had receded to a place that most people do not understand, because they've never been there.

This room was a testament to the insanity that had descended on our father. Dad needed help—more, I think, than any of us in the family could offer him.

"I see ya come to your senses, Marilynn," Dad said, his speech slightly slurred.

Mom didn't say anything. She just stared up at him. I could feel her trembling beside me.

I remembered all those homeless bums who wandered around Washington. "There but for the grace of God go I," Uncle Teddy had told me once as we watched one of the bag ladies walk by. "That's the old saying."

"What's it mean?" I'd asked Uncle Teddy.

"It means that anyone, no matter how strong they are, can lose their grip and descend into this madness," he'd said somberly. "Without God, we are lost."

I believed it, now. I really did.

"Tom, what are you doing here?" Mom said at last.

Dad grinned wide. "Purdy nice, ain't it? And cheap. Boy, is it dirt cheap."

"Tom, what are you *doing* here?" Mom repeated.

"It seemed like the logical place," Dad shrugged. "Nobody here to bother me. No rent, plenty of peace and quiet. The perfect place."

"It's no place for a child," Mom said softly, risking a quick glance toward her daughter. I saw Karen flinch a little.

"It ain't so bad," Dad said quickly. "A little work to

fix the place up, be good as new."

"I don't think so, Tom," Mom said firmly.

I saw my dad stiffen. He gripped the arms on the sofa chair and leaned forward a little.

"It is if I say so," he sneered. "Ain't nothin' you or anyone else can do about it."

"Tom, why don't you let me take Karen home?" Mom said.

"This is where she belongs," Dad said. "Here with me."

"This is no place for a child," Mom said again. "She needs a proper home."

Dad laughed. It was a harsh, guttural thing. "Yeah, sure. A *proper* home. What's that? Somethin' comes along and wipes that out, whatcha got? Nothin', that's what. Believe me, I know."

Mom let go of my hand. "Tom, I know you're in pain. I know that. But we can help. We really can. Just let us help you—"

"I don't need no stinkin' help!" Dad said angrily, rising from his throne.

"Tom, we can find people to help," Mom said, taking a step closer to the platform.

"Don't need it," he said, his voice almost a whimper. He sank back into the chair. "Don't want it."

My feet felt like they were glued to the floor. I was absolutely dumbfounded at the way Dad was going from high to low, from one extreme to the next. First he roars, then he whimpers. It was scary.

"Tom, you know that you can ride back with us," Mom said. "You know that."

I could see Dad's lip curl. "I ain't livin' up in Wash'ton. No way."

"There are people there who can help you," Mom persisted.

"Look, I tole ya," Dad said. "I don't need no help. I'm just fine and dandy. Just need a little investment to get me started, that's all."

"Do you need money?" Mom asked. "Would that help?"

"I could use a loaner," Dad said slyly. It made my stomach turn.

Mom reached into her purse. "Why don't you let Karen come on down from there, and I'll write you a check—"

"No!" Dad bellowed. "Karen's stayin' here with me. You go ahead and write that check, but she ain't goin' nowhere."

Mom closed her eyes. I was sure she was praying. I was too, in my own way. *Dear God*, I thought, *please help my dad. Please help our family get out of this deep, dark abyss. You are the only one who can help us now.*

After a little while, Mom opened her eyes. I could see in an instant that she was calmer and more determined. She wasn't walking away from here without Karen.

"Tom, what do you *really* want? Just tell me," Mom said. "What do you really want?"

Dad started crying. I don't think I'd ever seen him cry before. "I just want it the way it was before," he said huskily.

"But it can't be," Mom answered. "It won't be. You have to accept that."

"I *won't!*" he said.

"Tom, look around you," Mom said firmly. "Look

around. This place has been shut down for years. Your job is gone. The things you had before, they're all gone . . . "

"No, they ain't," Dad said, his head jerking toward Karen. "I still got y'all."

"Tom, no, you don't," Mom said quietly. "We've all moved to Washington. We've started a new life there."

"Don't care," Dad said, sniffing hard.

"Yes, you do," Mom said. "I know, deep in your heart, you *do* care. You care about your kids, about Cally, and Jana, and Karen, and Chris, and John, and Susan, and Timmy. I know that you only want the best for them."

For the first time since we'd arrived, Dad didn't answer back. He was listening, so Mom pressed forward.

"I know you want things to be the way they were before, but they can't be. Life moves on. It moves forward. And you have to move with it. That's just the way it is."

"You could move back," Dad said.

"You know I can't," Mom said.

"You could if you wanted to," he persisted.

"Tom, it's time to get on with our lives," she said. "It's time you got on with your life."

Dad hung his head low, resting it in both hands. Karen moved in beside him and stroked his unkempt hair. "It'll be okay," Karen said to him softly. "Really, it will be."

Dad stayed there like that, his head bowed, for the longest time. Mom and I glanced at each other, but we didn't say anything. Dad was so unpredictable, it was hard to imagine what he might do next.

He looked up, finally, and wiped away the tears on his face with his sleeves and the backs of his hands. "You can write that check now," he said gruffly.

"Only if you promise to get some help, some professional help," Mom answered back right away.

"Don't need no help," he said testily.

"Yes, you do," Mom said. "Promise me you'll go get some? If I talk to some people here, promise me you'll go see them?"

Dad glowered at us for a second. Suddenly, he broke into a huge, sly grin. "Ah, sure, why not?" he said. "What's the harm? What can they do to me?"

"They can help," Mom said. "That's what they can do. They can help."

"If you say so, Marilynn, I'll believe it," Dad said, settling back into his sofa chair. He barely even moved his hand to accept the check that Mom wrote and handed to him.

Karen let go of her father and took a tentative step away from him. Dad didn't say anything, so she took two more steps away from him.

"See you later, Daddy," she said, looking over one shoulder at him.

Dad didn't say anything. He was just staring blankly into space.

"Come on, Karen, honey," Mom said, moving toward her daughter. They met at the bottom of the steps and embraced. Neither said anything for the longest time.

"I'm ready now," Karen said.

"Then let's go home," Mom said. "The family's waiting for us."